She had let down her defenses, had thawed. Leo was nothing at all like any of the men she had ever met in her entire life.

"What are you doing?" Brianna asked weakly.

"I'm touching you. Do you want me to stop?"

"This is crazy."

"This is taking a chance."

"I don't even...know you...."

No, she certainly didn't. And yet, strangely, she knew more about him than any other woman did. Not that there was any point in getting tied down with semantics. "What does that have to do with wanting someone?" His voice was a low murmur in her ear and as he slid his hand along her waist, she could feel all rational thought disappearing.

So, she thought, fighting down the temptation to moan as his fingers continued to stroke her bare skin, he wasn't going to be sticking around. He was as nomadic as she was rooted to this place. But wasn't that what taking chances was all about?

All about the author...
Cathy Williams

CATHY WILLIAMS was born in the West Indies and has been writing Harlequin® romances for some fifteen years. She is a great believer in the power of perseverance as she had never written anything before (apart from school essays a lifetime ago!), and from the starting point of zero has now fulfilled her ambition to pursue this most enjoyable of careers. She would encourage any would-be writer to have faith and go for it! She lives in the beautiful Warwickshire countryside with her husband and three children, Charlotte, Olivia and Emma. When not writing she is hard-pressed to find a moment's free time in between the millions of household chores, not to mention being a one-woman taxi service for her daughters' never-ending social lives. She derives inspiration from the hot, lazy, tropical island of Trinidad (where she was born), from the peaceful countryside of middle England and, of course, from her many friends, who are a rich source of plots and are particularly garrulous when it comes to describing Harlequin Presents heroes. It would seem, from their complaints, that tall, dark and charismatic men are way too few and far between! Her hope is to continue writing romance fiction and providing those eternal tales of love for which, she feels, we all strive.

Other titles by Cathy Williams available in ebook:

ENTHRALLED BY MORETTI
HIS TEMPORARY MISTRESS
A DEAL WITH DI CAPUA
THE SECRET CASELLA BABY

Cathy Williams

——

Secrets of a Ruthless Tycoon

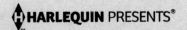

Recycling programs
for this product may
not exist in your area.

ISBN-13: 978-0-373-13720-6

SECRETS OF A RUTHLESS TYCOON

First North American Publication 2014

Copyright © 2014 by Cathy Williams

Printed in U.S.A.

Secrets of a Ruthless Tycoon

CHAPTER ONE

IN THE DIMINISHING light, Leo Spencer was beginning to question his decision to make this trip. He looked up briefly from the report blinking at him on his laptop and frowned at the sprawling acres of countryside reaching out on either side to distant horizons which had now been swallowed up by the gathering dusk.

It was on the tip of his tongue to tell his driver to put his foot down, but what would be the point? How much speed would Harry be able to pick up on these winding, unlit country roads, still hazardous from the recent bout of snow which was only now beginning to melt? The last thing he needed was to end up in a ditch somewhere. The last car they had passed had been several miles back. God only knew where the nearest town was.

He concluded that February was, possibly, the very worst month in which to have undertaken this trip to the outer reaches of Ireland. He had failed to foresee the length of time it would take to get to his destination and he now cursed the contorted reasoning that had made him reject the option of flying there on the company plane.

The flight to Dublin had been straightforward enough but, the minute he had met his driver outside the airport, the trip had evolved into a nightmare of traffic, diversions and, as they'd appeared to leave all traces of civilisation behind, a network of bleak, perilous roads made all the more threatening by the constant threat of snow. It hung in the air like a death shroud, biding its time for just the right unsuspecting mug to come along.

Giving up on all hope of getting anything useful done, Leo snapped shut his laptop and stared at the gloomy scenery.

The rolling hills were dark contours rising ominously up from flat fields in which lurked a honeycomb network of lakes, meandering streams and rivers, none of which was visible at this time of the late afternoon. Leo was accustomed to the almost constant artificial light of London. He had never had much time for the joys of the countryside and his indifference to it was rapidly being cemented with each passing mile.

But this was a trip that had to be undertaken.

When he reflected on the narrative of his life, he knew that it was an essential journey. The death of his mother eight months previously—

following so shortly after his father's own unexpected demise from a heart attack whilst, of all things, he had been playing golf with his friends—had left him with no excuses for avoidance. He had to find out where he really came from, who his real birth parents were. He would never have disrespected his adoptive parents when they were alive by searching out his birth family but the time had come.

He closed his eyes and the image of his own life flickered in front of him like an old-fashioned movie reel: adopted at birth by a successful and wealthy couple in their late thirties who had been unable to have children of their own; brought up with all the advantages a solid, middle-class background had to offer; private school and holidays abroad. A brilliant academic career followed by a stint at an investment bank which had been the springboard for a meteoric rise through the financial world until, at the ripe old age of thirty-two, he now had more money than he could ever hope to spend in a lifetime and the freedom to use it in the more creative arena of acquisitions.

He seemed to possess the golden touch. None of his acquisitions to date had failed. Additionally, he had been bequeathed a sizeable fortune by his parents. All told, the only grey area in a life that had been blessed with success was the murky blur of his true heritage. Like a pernicious weed, it had never been completely uprooted. Curiosity had always been there, hovering on the edges of his consciousness, and he knew that it would always be there unless he took active measures to put it to rest once and for all.

Not given to introspection of any sort, there were moments when he suspected that it had left a far-reaching legacy, despite all the advantages his wonderful adoptive parents had given him. His relationships with women had all been short-lived. He enjoyed a varied love life with some of the most beautiful and eligible women on the London scene, yet the thought of committing to any of them had always left him cold. He always used the excuse of being the kind of man whose commitment to work left little fertile ground on which a successful relationship could flourish. But there lurked the nagging suspicion that the notion of his own feckless parents dumping him on whatever passing strangers they could had fostered a deep-seated mistrust of any form of permanence, despite the sterling example his adoptive parents had set for him.

He had known for several years where he could locate his mother. He had no idea if his natural father was still on the scene—quite possibly not. The whereabouts of his mother was information that had sat, untouched, in his locked office drawer until now.

He had taken a week off work, informing his secretary that he would be contactable at all times by email or on his mobile phone. He would find his mother, make his own judgements and he would leave, putting to rest the curiosity that had plagued him over the years. He had a good idea of what he would find but it would be useful having his suspicions confirmed. He wasn't looking for answers or touching reconciliations. He was looking for closure.

And, naturally, he had no intention of letting her know his identity. He was sinfully rich and there was nothing like money to engender all the wrong responses. There was no way he intended to have some irresponsible deadbeat who had given him up for adoption holding out a begging bowl and suddenly claiming parental love—not to mention whatever half- siblings he had who would feel free to board the gravy train.

His mouth curled derisively at the mere thought of it.

'Any chance we could actually get this car into fifth gear?' he asked Harry, who caught his eye in the rear-view mirror and raised his eyebrows.

'Aren't you appreciating the wonderful scenery, sir?'

'You've been with me for eight years, Harry.

Have I ever given any indication that I like the countryside?' Harry, strangely, was the only one in whom Leo had confided. They shared an uncommonly strong bond. Leo would have trusted his driver with his life. He certainly trusted him with thoughts he never would have shared with another living soul.

'There's always a first, sir,' Harry suggested calmly. 'And, no, there is no way I can drive any faster. Not on these roads. And have you noticed the sky?'

'In passing.'

'Snow's on the way, sir.'

'And I'm hoping that it will delay its arrival until I'm through…doing what I have to do.' From where he was sitting, it was hard to see where the sky met the open land. It was all just a black, formless density around them. Aside from the sound of the powerful engine of the car, the silence was so complete that, with eyes closed, anyone could be forgiven for thinking that they were suffering sensory deprivation.

'The weather is seldom obedient, sir. Even for a man like yourself who is accustomed to having his orders obeyed.'

Leo grinned. 'You talk too much, Harry.'

'So my better half often tells me, sir. Are you certain you don't require my services when we reach Ballybay?'

'Quite certain. You can get a cab driver to deliver the car back to London and the company plane will return you to your better half. I've alerted my secretary to have it on standby; she'll text you where. Make sure you tell my people to have it ready and waiting for when I need to return to London. I have no intention of repeating this journey by car any time soon.'

'Of course, sir.'

Leo flipped back open the laptop and consigned all wayward thoughts of what he would find when he finally arrived to the furthermost outer reaches of his mind. Losing yourself in pointless speculation was a waste of time.

It was two hours by the time he was informed that they were in Ballybay. Either he had missed the main part of the town or else there was nothing much to it. He could just about make out the vast stillness of a lake and then a scattering of houses and shops nestling amidst the hills and dales.

'Is this it?' he asked Harry, who tut-tutted in response.

'Were you expecting Oxford Street, sir?'

'I was expecting a little more by way of life. Is there even a hotel?' He frowned and thought that allowing a week off work might have been over- estimating the time he would need. A couple of days at most should see him conclude his business.

'There's a pub, sir.'

Leo followed his driver's pointing finger and made out an ancient pub that optimistically boasted 'vacancies'. He wondered what the passing tourist trade could possibly be in a town that time appeared to have forgotten.

'Drop me off here, Harry, and you can head off.' He was travelling light: one holdall, suitably battered, into which he now stuffed his slim laptop.

Already, he was making comparisons between what appeared to be this tiny town of splendid isolation and the completely different backdrop to life with his adoptive parents. The busy Surrey village in which he had been brought up buzzed with a veritable treasure trove of trendy gastropubs and designer shops. The landscape was confined and neatly manicured. The commuter links to London were excellent and that was reflected in the high-end property market. Gated mansions were hidden from prying eyes by long drives. On Saturdays, the high street was bursting with expensive people who lived in the expensive houses and drove the expensive cars.

He stepped out of the Range Rover to a gusty wind and freezing cold.

The ancient pub looked decidedly more inviting given the temperatures outside and he strode towards it without hesitation.

Inside the pub, Brianna Sullivan was nursing an incipient headache. Even in the depths of winter, Friday nights brought in the crowds and, whilst she was grateful for their patronage, she yearned for peace and quiet. Both seemed about as elusive as finding gold dust in the kitchen sink. She had inherited this pub from her father nearly six years ago and there were no allowances made for time out. There was just her, and it was her livelihood. Choice didn't feature heavily on the menu.

'Tell Pat he can come and get his own drinks at the bar,' she hissed to Shannon. 'We're busy enough here without you carrying trays of drinks over to him because he broke his leg six months ago. He's perfectly capable of getting them himself, or else he can send that brother of his over to get them.' At one end of the bar, Aidan and two of his friends were beginning to sing a rousing love song to grab her attention.

'I'll have to chuck you out for unruly behaviour,' she snapped at Aidan as she slid refills for them along the counter.

'You know you love me, darling.'

Brianna shot him an exasperated look and told him that he either settled his tab in full, right here and right now, or else that was the last pint he was going to get.

She needed more people behind the bar but what on earth would she do with them on the week days, when the place was less rowdy and busy? How could she justify the expenditure? And yet, she barely had enough time to function properly. Between the bookkeeping, the stock taking, the ordering and the actual standing behind the bar every night, time—the one thing she didn't have—was galloping past. She was twenty-seven years old and in the blink of an eye she would be thirty, then forty, then fifty, and still doing the things she was doing now, still struggling to kick back. She was young but, hell, she felt old a lot of the time.

Aidan continued to try his banter on her but she blocked him out. Now that she had begun feeling sorry for herself, she was barely aware of what was going on around her.

Surely her years at university had not equipped her to spend the rest of her life running this pub? She loved her friends and the tight-knit community but surely she was entitled to just have some *fun*? Six months of fun was all she had had when she had finished university, then it had been back here to help look after her father who had managed to drink himself into a premature grave.

Not a day went by when she didn't miss him.

For twelve years after her mother had died it had been just the two of them, and she missed his easy laughter, his support, his corny jokes. She wondered how he would feel if he knew that she was still here, at the pub. He had always wanted her to fly away and develop a career in art, but then little had he known that he would not be around to make that possible.

She only became aware that something was different when, still absorbed in her own thoughts, it dawned on her that the bar had grown silent.

In the act of pulling a pint, she raised her eyes and there, framed in the doorway, was one of the most startlingly beautiful men she had ever seen in her life. Tall, windswept dark hair raked back from a face that was shamefully good-looking. He didn't seem in the slightest taken aback by the fact that all eyes were on him as he looked around, his midnight-black eyes finally coming to rest on her.

Brianna felt her cheeks burn at the casual inspection, then she returned to what she was doing and so did everyone else. The noise levels once again rose and the jokes resumed; old Connor did his usual and began singing lustily and drunkenly until he was laughed down.

She ignored the stranger, yet was all too aware of his presence, and not at all surprised that when she next glanced up it was to find him standing right in front of her.

'The sign outside says that there are vacancies.' Leo practically had to shout to make himself heard above the noise. The entire town seemed to have congregated in this small pub. Most of the green leather stools assembled along the bar were filled, as were the tables. Behind the bar, two girls were trying hard to keep up with the demands—a small, busty brunette and the one in front of whom he was now standing. A tall, slender girl with copper-coloured hair which she had swept up into a rough pony tail and, as she looked at him, the clearest, greenest eyes he had ever seen.

'Why do you want to know?' Brianna asked.

His voice matched the rest of him. It was deep and lazy and induced an annoying, fluttery feeling in the pit of her stomach. 'Why do you think? I need to rent a room and I take it this is the only place in the village that rents rooms…?'

'Is it not good enough for you?'

'Where's the owner?'

'You're looking at her.'

He did, much more thoroughly this time. Bare of any make-up, her skin was satin-smooth and creamy white. There was not a freckle in sight, despite the vibrant colour of her hair. She was wearing a pair of faded jeans and a long-sleeved jumper but neither detracted from her looks.

'Right. I need a room.'

'I will show you up to one just as soon as I get a free moment. In the meantime, would you like something to drink?' What on earth was this man doing here? He certainly wasn't from around these parts, nor did he know anyone around here. She would know. It was a tiny community; they all knew each other in some way, shape or form.

'What I'd like is a hot shower and a good night's sleep.'

'Both will have to wait, Mr…?'

'My name is Leo and, if you give me a key and point me in the right direction, I'll make my own way upstairs. And, by the way, is there anywhere to eat around here?'

Not only was the man a stranger but he was an obnoxious one. Brianna could feel her hackles rising. Memories of another good-looking, well-spoken stranger rose unbidden to the foreground. As learning curves went, she had been taught well what sort of men to avoid.

'You'll have to go into Monaghan for that,' she informed him shortly. 'I can fix you a sandwich but—'

'Yes—but I'll have to wait because you're too busy behind the bar. Forget the food. If you need a deposit, tell me how much and then you can give me the key.'

Brianna shot him an impatient glance and called over to Aidan. 'Take the reins,' she told him. 'And no free drinks. I've got to show this man to a room. I'll be back down in five minutes, and if I find out that you've helped yourself to so much as a thimble of free beer I'll ban you for a week.'

'Love you too, Brianna.'

'How long would you be wanting the room for?' was the first thing she asked him as soon as they were out of the bar area and heading upstairs. She was very much aware of him following her and she could feel the hairs on the back of her neck rising. Had she lived so long in this place that the mere sight of a halfway decent guy was enough to bring her out in a cold sweat?

'A few days.' She was as graceful as a dancer and he was tempted to ask why a girl with her looks was running a pub in the middle of nowhere. Certainly not for the stress-free existence. She looked hassled and he could understand that if it was as busy every night of the week.

'And might I ask what brings you to this lovely part of Ireland?' She pushed open the door to one of the four rooms she rented out and stood back, allowing him to brush past her.

Leo took his time looking around him. It was

small but clean. He would have to be sharp-witted when it came to avoiding the beams but it would do. He turned round to her and began removing his coat which he tossed onto the high-backed wooden chair by the dressing table.

Brianna took a step back. The room was small and he seemed to over-power it with his presence. She was treated to a full view of his muscular body now he was without his coat: black jeans, a black jumper and the sort of olive-brown complexion that told her that, somewhere along the line, there was a strain of exotic blood running through him.

'You can ask,' Leo agreed. Billionaire searching for his long-lost, feckless parent wasn't going to cut it. One hint of that and it would be round the grapevine faster than he could pay her the deposit on the room; of that he was convinced. Checking his mother out was going to be an incognito exercise and he certainly wasn't going to be ambushed by a pub owner with a loose tongue, however pretty she was.

'But you're not going to tell me. Fair enough.' She shrugged. 'If you want breakfast, it's served between seven and eight. I run this place single-handed so I don't have a great deal of time to wait on guests.'

'Such a warm welcome.'

Brianna flushed and belatedly remembered

that he was a paying guest and not another of the lads downstairs to whom she was allowed to give as good as she got. 'I apologise if I seem rude, Mr…'

'Leo.'

'But I'm rushed off my feet at the moment and not in the best of moods. The bathroom is through there…' She pointed in the direction of a white-washed door. 'And there are tea- and coffee-making facilities.' She backed towards the door, although she was finding it hard to tear her eyes away from his face.

If he brought to mind unhappy memories of Daniel Fluke, then it could be said that he was a decidedly more threatening version: bigger, better looking and without the readily charming patter, and that in itself somehow felt more dangerous. And she still had no idea what he was doing in this part of the world.

'If you could settle the deposit on the room…' She cleared her throat and watched in silence as he extracted a wad of notes from his wallet and handed her the required amount.

'And tell me, what is there to do here?' he asked, shoving his hands in his pockets and tilting his head to one side. 'I guess you must know everything…and everyone?'

'You've picked a poor time of year for sightseeing, Mr…eh…Leo. I'm afraid walking might be a little challenging, especially as snow is predicted, and you can forget about the fishing.'

'Perhaps I'll just explore the town,' he murmured. Truly amazing eyes, he thought. Eyelashes long and dark and in striking contrast to the paleness of her skin. 'I hope I'm not making you nervous… Sorry, you didn't tell me your name, although I gather it's Brianna…?'

'We don't get very many strangers in this part of town, certainly not in the depths of winter.'

'And now you're renting a room to one and you don't know what he does or why he's here in the first place. Understandable if you feel a little edgy…' He shot her a crooked smile and waited for it to take effect; waited to see her loosen up, smile back in return, look him up and down covertly; waited for the impact he knew he had on women to register. Nothing. She frowned and looked at him coolly, clearly assessing him.

'That's right.' Brianna folded her arms and leaned against the doorframe.

'I…' He realised that he hadn't banked on this. He actually hadn't expected the place to be so small. Whilst he had acknowledged that he couldn't just show up on his mother's doorstep and do his character assessment on the spot, he was now realising that the other option of extracting information from random drinkers at some faceless, characterless bar close to where the woman lived was quite likely also out of the question.

'Yes?' Brianna continued to look at him. She might be grateful for the money—it wasn't as though people were falling over themselves to rent a room in the depths of winter—but on the other hand she *was* a single woman, here on her own, and what if he turned out to be a homicidal maniac?

Granted it was unlikely that a homicidal maniac would announce his intentions because she happened to ask, but if he seemed too shifty, just too untrustworthy, then she would send him on his way, money or not.

'I'm not proud of this.' Leo glanced around him. His gaze settled on an exquisite watercolour painting above the bed and moved to the row of books neatly stacked on the shelf just alongside it. 'But I jacked in a perfectly good job a fortnight ago.'

'A perfectly good job doing what?' Brianna knew that she was giving him the third degree; that he was under no obligation to explain himself to her; that she could lose trade should he choose to spread the word that the landlady at the Angler's Catch was the sort who gave her customers a hard time. She also knew that there was a fair to middling chance that Aidan had already had a couple of free whiskies at her expense, and that

Shannon would be running around like a headless chicken trying to fill orders, but her feet refused to budge. She was riveted by the sight of his dark, handsome face, glued to the spot by that lazy, mesmerising drawl.

'Working at one of those big, soulless companies...' Which was not, strictly speaking, a complete lie, although it had to be said that his company was less soulless than most. 'Decided that I would try my luck at something else. I've always wanted to...write, so I'm in the process of taking a little time out to try my hand at it; see where that takes me...' He strolled towards the window and peered out. 'I thought a good place to start would be Ireland. It's noted for its inspiring scenery, isn't it? Thought I would get a flavour of the country...the bits most people don't see; thought I would set my book here...'

He glanced over his shoulder to her before resuming his thoughtful contemplation of the very little he could actually see in the almost complete, abysmal darkness outside. 'The weather has knocked my progress off a little, hence—' he raised his shoulders in a rueful, elegant shrug '—here I am.'

A budding author? Surely not. He certainly didn't *look* like one, yet why on earth would he lie? The fact that he had held down a conventional job no doubt accounted for that hint of *sophisti-*

cation she was getting; something intangible that emanated from him, an air of unspoken authority that she found difficult to quite define but…

Brianna felt herself thaw. 'It gets a little quieter towards the end of the evening,' she offered. 'If you haven't fallen asleep, I can make you something to eat.'

'That's very kind of you,' Leo murmured. The passing guilt he had felt at having to concoct a lie was rationalised, justified and consigned to oblivion. He had responded creatively to an unexpected development.

Getting her onside could also work in his favour. Publicans knew everything about everyone and were seldom averse to a bit of healthy gossip. Doubtless he would be able to extract some background information on his mother and, when he had that information, he would pay her a visit in the guise of someone doing business in the area—maybe interviewing her for the fictitious book he had supposedly jacked his job in for. He would add whatever he learnt to whatever he saw and would get a complete picture of the woman who had abandoned him at birth. He would get his closure. The unfinished mosaic of his life would finally have all the pieces welded together.

'Right, then…' Brianna dithered awkwardly. 'Is there anything you need to know about…the room? How the television works? How you can get an outside line?'

'I think I can figure both out,' Leo responded dryly. 'You can get back to your rowdy crew in the bar.'

'They are, aren't they?' She laughed softly and hooked her thumbs into the pockets of her jeans.

Without warning, Leo felt a jolt of unexpected arousal at the sight. She was very slender. Her figure was almost boyish, not at all like the women he was routinely attracted to, whose assets were always far more prominent and much more aggressively advertised; beautiful, overtly sexy women who had no time for downplaying what they possessed.

He frowned at his body's unexpected lapse in self-control. 'You should employ more people to help you out,' he told her abruptly.

'Perhaps I should.' Just like that she felt the change in the atmosphere and she reminded herself that, writer or not, guys who were too sexy for their own good spelled trouble. She reminded herself of how easy it was to be taken in by what was on the outside, only to completely miss the ugly stuff that was buried underneath.

She coolly excused herself and returned to find that, just as expected, Aidan was knocking back a glass of whisky which he hurriedly banged on the counter the second he spotted her approaching.

Shannon appeared to be on the verge of tears and, despite what Brianna had told her, was scuttling over with a tray of drinks to the group of high-spirited men at the corner table, most of whom they had gone to school with, which Brianna thought was no reason for them to think they could get waitress service. Old Connor, with several more drinks inside him, was once again attempting to be a crooner but could scarcely enunciate the words to the song he was trying to belt out.

It was the same old same old, and she felt every day of her twenty-seven years by the time they all began drifting off into an unwelcoming night. Twenty-seven years old and she felt like forty-seven. The snow which had thankfully disappeared for the past week had returned to pay them another visit, and outside the flakes were big and fat under the street lights.

Shannon was the last to leave and Brianna had to chivvy her along. For a young girl of nineteen, she had a highly developed mothering instinct and worried incessantly about her friend living above the pub on her own.

'Although at least there's a strapping man there with you tonight!' She laughed, wrapping her scarf around her neck and winking.

'From my experience of the opposite sex...' Brianna grinned back and shouted into the darkness with a wave '…they're the first to dive for cover if there's any chance of danger—and that includes the strapping ones!'

'Then you've just met the wrong men.'

She spun round to see Leo standing by the bar, arms folded, his dark eyes amused. He had showered and changed and was in a pair of jeans and a cream, thickly knitted jumper which did dramatic things for his colouring.

'You've come for your sandwich.' She tore her eyes away from him and quickly and efficiently began clearing the tables, getting the brunt of the work done before she had to get up at seven the following morning.

'I gathered that the crowd was beginning to disperse. The singing had stopped.' He began giving her a hand.

Clearing tables was a novel experience. When he happened to be in the country, he ate out. On the rare occasions when he chose to eat in, he ate food specially prepared for him by his housekeeper, who was also an excellent chef. She cooked for him, discreetly waited until he was finished and then cleared the table. Once a month, she cooked for both him and Harry and these meals were usually pre-planned to coincide with a football game. They would eat, enjoy a couple of beers and watch the football. It was his most perfect down time.

He wondered when and how that small slice of normality, the normality of clearing a table, had vanished—but then was it so surprising? He ran multi-million-pound companies that stretched across the world. Normality, as most people understood it, was in scarce supply.

'You really don't have to help,' Brianna told him as she began to fetch the components for a sandwich. 'You're a paying guest.'

'With a curious mind. Tell me about the wannabe opera singer…'

He watched as she worked, making him a sandwich that could have fed four, tidying away the beer mugs and glasses into the industrial-sized dishwasher. He listened keenly as she chatted, awkwardly at first, but then fluently, about all the regulars—laughing at their idiosyncrasies; relating little anecdotes of angry wives showing up to drag their other halves back home when they had abused the freedom pass they had been given for a couple of hours.

'Terrific sandwich, by the way.' It had been. Surprisingly so, bearing in mind that the sandwiches he occasionally ate were usually ornate affairs with intricate fillings prepared by top chefs in expensive restaurants. He lifted the plate as she wiped clean the counter underneath. 'I'm guessing that you pretty much know everyone who lives around here…'

'You guess correctly.'

'One of the upsides of living in a small place?' He could think of nothing worse. He thoroughly enjoyed the anonymity of big-city life.

'It's nice knowing who your neighbours are. It's a small population here. 'Course, some of them have gone to live in other parts of Ireland, and a few really daring ones have moved to your part of the world, but on the whole, yes, we all know each other.'

She met his steady gaze and again felt that hectic bloom of colour invade her cheeks. 'Nearly everyone here tonight were regulars. They've been coming here since my dad owned the place.'

'And your dad is…?'

'Dead,' Brianna said shortly. 'Hence this is now my place.'

'I'm sorry. Tough work.'

'I can handle it.' She took his plate, stuck it into the sink then washed her hands.

'And, of course, you have all your friends around you for support… Siblings as well? What about your mother?'

'Why are you asking me all these questions?'

'Aren't we always curious about people we've never met and places we've never seen? As a… writer you could say that I'm more curious than most.' He stood up and began walking towards the door through which lay the stairs up to his bedroom. 'If you think I'm being too nosy then tell me.'

Brianna half-opened her mouth with a cool retort, something that would restore the balance between paying guest and landlady, but the temptation to chat to a new face, a new person, someone who didn't know her from time immemorial, was too persuasive.

A writer! How wonderful to meet someone on the same wavelength as her! What would it hurt to drop her guard for a couple of days and give him the benefit of the doubt? He might be good-looking but he wasn't Danny Fluke.

'You're not nosy.' She smiled tentatively. 'I just don't understand why you're interested. We're a pretty run-of-the-mill lot here; I can't imagine you would get anything useful for your book.' She couldn't quite make him out. He was in shadow, lounging indolently against the wall as he looked at her. She squashed the uneasy feeling that there was more to him than met the eye.

'People's stories interest me.' He pushed himself away from the wall and smiled. 'You'd be surprised what you can pick up; what you can find…useful.' There was something defiant yet vulnerable about her. It was an appealing mix and a refreshing change from the women he normally met.

'Tomorrow,' he said, 'Point me in the direction

of what to do and you can relax. Tell me about
the people who live here.'

'Don't be crazy. You're a guest. You're paying for your bed and board and, much as I'd love
to swap the room for your labour, I just can't afford it.'

'And I wouldn't dream of asking.' He wondered how she would react if she knew that he
could buy this pub a hundred times over and it
would still only be loose change to him. He wondered what she would say if she knew that, in between the stories she had to tell, there would be
that vital one he wanted to hear. 'No, you'd be
helping me out, giving me one or two ideas. Plus
you look as though you could use a day off...'

The thought of putting her feet up for a couple
of hours dangled in front of her like the promise
of a banquet to a starving man. 'I can work and
chat at the same time,' she conceded. 'And it'll
be nice to have someone lend a hand.'

CHAPTER TWO

BRIANNA WOKE AT six the following morning to furious snowfall. Outside, it was as still as a tomb. On days like this, her enjoyment of the peace and quiet was marred by the reality that she would have next to no customers, but then she thought of the stranger lying in the room down from hers on the middle floor. Leo. He hadn't baulked at the cost of the room and, the evening before, had insisted on paying her generously for an evening meal. Some of her lost income would be recovered.

And then…the unexpected, passing companionship of a fellow artiste. She knew most of the guys her age in the village and it had to be said that there wasn't a creative streak to be found among the pack of them.

She closed her eyes and luxuriated for a few stolen minutes, just thinking about him. When she thought about the way his dark eyes had followed her as she had tidied and chatted, wiped the bar counter and straightened the stools, she could feel the heat rush all through her body until it felt as though it was on fire.

She hadn't had a boyfriend in years.

The appearance of the stranger was a stark reminder of how her emotional life had ground to a standstill after her disastrous relationship with Daniel Fluke at university. All those years ago, she had fancied herself in love.

Daniel had been the complete package: gorgeous, with chestnut-brown hair, laughing blue eyes and an abundance of pure charm that had won him a lot of admirers. But he had only had eyes for her. They had been an item for nearly two years. He had met her father; had sat at the very bar downstairs, nursing a pint with him. He had been studying law and had possessed that peculiar surety of someone who has always known what road they intended to go down. His father was a retired judge, his mother a key barrister in London. They were all originally from Dublin, one of those families with textbook, aristocratic genealogy. They still kept a fabulous apartment in Dublin, but he had lived in London since he had been a child.

Looking back, Brianna could see that there had always been the unspoken assumption that she should consider herself lucky to have nabbed him, that a guy like him could have had any pretty girl on campus. At the time, though, she had walked around with her head in the clouds. She had actually thought that their relationship was built to last. Even now, years after the event, she could still taste the bitterness in her mouth when she remembered how it had all ended.

She had been swept off her feet on a post-graduation holiday in New Zealand, all expenses paid. She shuddered now when she thought back to the ease with which she had accepted his generosity. She had returned to Ireland only to discover that her father was seriously ill and, at that point, she had made the mistake of showing her hand. She had made the fatal error of assuming that Daniel would be right there by her side, supporting her through tough times.

'Of course,' he had told her, 'There's no way I can stay there with you. I have an internship due to start in London…'

She had understood. She had hoped for weekends. Her father would recover, she had insisted, choosing to misread the very clear messages the doctors had been giving her about his prognosis. And, when he did, she would join him in London. There would be loads of opportunities for her in the city and they would easily be able to afford a place to rent. There would be no need to rush to buy…not until they were ready really to seal their relationship. Plus, it would be a wonderful time for her finally to meet his family: the brother he spoke so much about, who did clever things in banking, and his kid sister who was at a boarding school in Gloucester. And of course his parents, who never seemed to be in one place for very long.

She had stupidly made assumptions about a future that had never been on the cards. They had been at university together and, hell, it had been a lot of fun. She was by far the fittest girl there. But a future together…?

The look of embarrassed, dawning horror on his face had said it all but still, like the young fool she had been, she had clung on and asked for explanations. The more he had been forced to explain, the cooler his voice had become. They were worlds apart; how could she seriously have thought that they would end up *married*? Wasn't it enough that she had had an all-expenses-paid farewell holiday? He was expected to marry a certain type of woman…that was just the way it was…she should just stop clinging and move on…

She'd moved on but still a part of her had remained rooted to that moment in time. Why else had she made no effort to get her love life back on track?

The stranger's unexpected arrival on the scene had opened Pandora's box in her head and, much as she wanted to slam the lid back down, she remained lying in bed for far longer than she should, just thinking.

It was after eight by the time she made it down to the bar, belatedly remembering the strict times during which her guest could have his breakfast. As landladies went, she would definitely not be in the running for a five-star rating.

She came to a halt by the kitchen door when she discovered that Leo was already there, appearing to make himself at home. There was a cup of coffee in front of him, and his laptop, which he instantly closed the second he looked up and spied her hovering in the doorway, a bit like a guest on her own premises.

'I hope you don't mind me making myself at home,' Leo said, pushing his chair back and folding his hands behind his head to look at her. 'I'm an early riser and staying in bed wasn't a tempting thought.' He had been up since six, in fact, and had already accomplished a great deal of work, although less than he had anticipated, because for once he had found his mind wandering to the girl now dithering in front of him. Was it because he was so completely removed from his comfort zone that his brain was not functioning with the rigid discipline to which it was accustomed? Was that why he had fallen asleep thinking of those startling green eyes and had awakened less than five hours later with a painful erection?

He might be willing to exploit whatever she knew about his mother, if she knew anything at all, but he certainly wasn't interested in progressing beyond that.

'You've been working.' Brianna smiled hesitantly. His impact on all her senses seemed as powerful in the clear light of day as it had been the night before. She galvanised herself into action and began unloading the dishwasher, stacking all the glasses to be returned to the bar outside; fetching things from the fridge so that she could make him the breakfast which was included in the money he had paid her.

'I have. I find that I work best in the mornings.'

'Have you managed to get anything down? I guess it must be quite an ordeal trying to get your imagination to do what you want it to do. Can I ask you what your book is going to be about? Or would you rather keep that to yourself?'

'People and the way they interact.' Leo hastened to get away from a topic in which he had no intention of becoming mired. The last time he had written anything that required the sort of imagination she was talking about had been at secondary school. 'Do you usually get up this early?'

'Earlier.' She refilled his mug and began cracking eggs, only pausing when he told her to sit down and talk to him for a few minutes rather than rushing into making breakfast.

Brianna blushed and obeyed. Nerves threatened to overwhelm her. She sneaked a glance at him and all over again was rendered breathless by the sheer force of his good looks and peculiar magnetism. 'There's a lot to do when you run a pub.' She launched into hurried speech to fill the silence. 'And, like I said, I'm doing it all on my own, so I have no one to share the responsibility with.'

Leo, never one to indulge his curiosity when it came to women—and knowing very well that, whatever information he was interested in gathering, certainly had nothing to do with *her* so why waste time hearing her out?—was reluctantly intrigued. 'A curious life you chose for yourself,' he murmured.

'I didn't choose it. *It* chose *me*.'

'Explain.'

'Are you really interested?'

'I wouldn't ask if I wasn't,' Leo said with a shrug. He had wondered whether she was really as pretty as he had imagined her to be. Subdued lighting in a pub could do flattering things to an average woman. He was discovering that his first impressions had been spot on. In fact, they had failed to do her justice. She had an ethereal, angelic beauty about her that drew the eye and compelled him to keep on staring. His eyes drifted slightly down to her breasts, small buds causing just the tiniest indentations in her unflattering, masculine jumper, which he guessed had belonged at one point to her father.

'My dad died unexpectedly. Well, maybe there were signs before. I didn't see them. I was at university, not getting back home as often as I knew I should, and Dad was never one to make a fuss when it came to his health.' She was startled at the ease with which she confessed to the guilt that had haunted her ever since her father had died. She could feel the full brunt of Leo's attention on her and it was as flattering as it was unnerving, not at all what she was accustomed to.

'He left a lot of debts.' She cleared her throat and blinked back the urge to cry. 'I think things must have slipped as he became ill and he never told me. The bank manager was very understanding but I had to keep running the pub so that I could repay the debts. I couldn't sell it, even though I tried for a while. There's a good summer trade here. Lots of fantastic scenery. Fishing. Brilliant walks. But the trade is a little seasonal and, well, the economy isn't great. I guess you'd know. You probably have to keep a firm rein on your finances if you've packed your job in…'

Leo flushed darkly and skirted around that ingenuous observation. 'So you've been here ever since,' he murmured. 'And no partner around to share the burden?'

'No.' Brianna looked down quickly and then stood up. 'I should get going with my chores. It's snowing outside and it looks like it's going to get worse, which usually means that the pub loses business, but just in case any hardy souls show up I can't have it looking a mess.'

So, he thought, there *had* been a man and it had ended badly. He wondered who the guy was. Some losers only stuck by their women when the times were good. The second the winds of change began blowing, they ran for the hills. He felt an unexpected spurt of anger towards this mystery person who had consigned her to a life on her own of drudgery, running a pub to make ends meet and pay off bills. He reined back his unruly mind and reminded himself that his primary purpose wasn't as counsellor but as information gatherer.

'If you really meant it about helping—and I promise I won't take advantage of your kind offer— you could try and clear a path through the snow, just in case it stops; at least my customers would be able to get to the door. It doesn't look promising…' She moved to one of the windows and frowned at the strengthening blizzard. 'What do you intend to do if the weather doesn't let up?' She turned to face him.

'It'll let up. I can't afford to stay here for very long.'

'You could always incorporate a snow storm in your book.'

'It's a thought.' He moved to stand next to her and at once he breathed in the fragrant, flowery smell of her hair which was, again, tied back in a pony tail. His fingers itched to release it, just to see how long it was, how thick. He noticed how she edged away slightly from him. 'I'll go see what I can do about the snow. You'll have to show me where the equipment is.'

'The equipment consists of a shovel and some bags of sand for gritting.' She laughed, putting a little more distance between them, because just for a second there she had felt short of breath with him standing so close to her.

'You do this yourself whenever it snows?' he asked, once the shovel was in his hand and the door to the pub thrown open to the elements. He thought of his last girlfriend, a model who didn't possess a pair of wellies to her name, and would only have gone near snow if it happened to be falling on a ski slope in Val d'Isere.

'Only if it looks as though it would make a difference. There've been times when I've wasted two hours trying to clear a path, only to stand back and watch the snow cover it all up in two minutes. You can't go out in those…er…jeans; you'll be soaked through. I don't suppose you brought any, um, waterproof clothing with you?'

Leo burst out laughing. 'Believe it or not, I didn't pack for a snow storm. The jeans will have to do. If they get soaked, they'll dry in front of that open fire in the lounge area.'

He worked out. He was strong. And yet he found that battling with the elements was exercise of a completely different sort. This was not the sanitised comfort of his expensive gym, with perfectly oiled machinery that was supposed to test the body to its limits. This was raw nature and, by the time he looked at his handiwork, a meagre path already filling up with fast falling snow, an hour and a half had flown past.

He had no gloves. His hands were freezing. But hell, it was invigorating. In fact, he had completely forgotten the reason why he was in this Godforsaken village in the first place. His thoughts were purely and utterly focused on trying to outsmart and out-shovel the falling snow.

The landscape had turned completely white. The pub was set a distance from the main part of the village and was surrounded by open fields. Pausing to stand back, his arm resting heavily on the shovel which he had planted firmly in the ground, he felt that he was looking at infinity. It evoked the strangest sensation of peace and awe, quite different from the irritation he had felt the day before when he had stared moodily out of the window at the tedium of never-ending fields and cursed his decision to get there by car.

He stayed out another hour, determined not to be beaten, but in the end he admitted defeat and returned to the warmth of the pub, to find the fire blazing and the smell of food wafting from the kitchen.

'I fought the snow...' God, he felt like a cave-man returning from a hard day out hunting. 'And the snow won. Don't bank on any customers today. Something smells good.'

'I don't normally do lunch for guests.'

'You'll be royally paid for your efforts.' He stifled a surge of irritation that the one thing most women would have given their eye teeth to do for him was something she clearly had done because she had had no choice. She was stuck with him. She could hardly expect him to starve because lunch wasn't included in the price of the room. 'You were going to fill me in on the people who live around here.' He reminded her coolly of the deal they had struck.

'It's not very exciting.' She looked at him and her heartbeat quickened. 'You're going to have to change. You're soaked through. If you give me your damp clothes, I can put them in front of the fire in the snug.'

'The snug?'

'My part of the house.' She leaned back against the kitchen counter, hands behind her. 'Self-contained quarters. Only small—two bedrooms, a little snug, a kitchen, bathroom and a study where Dad used to do all the accounts for the pub. It's where I grew up. I can remember loving it when the place was full and I could roam through the guest quarters bringing them cups of tea and coffee. It used to get a lot busier in the boom days.'

She certainly looked happy recounting those jolly times but, as far as Leo was concerned, it sounded like just the sort of restricted life that would have driven him crazy.

And yet, this could have been his fate—living in this tiny place where everyone knew everyone else. In fact, he wouldn't even have had the relative comforts of a village pub. He would probably have been dragged up in a hovel somewhere by the town junkie, because what other sort of loser gave away their own child? It was a sobering thought.

'I could rustle up some of Dad's old shirts for you. I kept quite a few for myself. I'll leave them outside your bedroom door and you can hand me the jeans so that I can launder them.'

She hadn't realised how lonely it was living

above the pub on her own, making every single decision on her own, until she was rummaging through her wardrobe, picking out shirts and enjoying the thought of having someone to lend them to, someone sharing her space, even if it was only in the guise of a guest who had been temporarily blown off-path by inclement weather.

She warmed at the thought of him trying and failing to clear the path to the pub of snow. When she gently knocked on his bedroom door ten minutes later, she was carrying a bundle of flannel shirts and thermal long-sleeved vests. She would leave them outside the door, and indeed she was bending down to do just that when the door opened.

She looked sideways and blinked rapidly at the sight of bare ankles. Bare ankles and strong calves, with dark hair… Her eyes drifted further upwards to bare thighs…lean, muscular bare thighs. Her mouth went dry. She was still clutching the clothes to her chest, as if shielding herself from the visual invasion of his body on her senses. His *semi-clad* body.

'Are these for me?'

Brianna snapped out of her trance and stared at him wordlessly.

'The clothes?' Leo arched an amused eyebrow as he took in her bright-red face and parted lips.

'They'll come in very handy. Naturally, you can put them on the tab.'

He was wearing boxers and nothing else. Brianna's brain registered that as a belated postscript. Most of her brain was wrapped up with stunned, shocked appreciation of his body. Broad shoulders and powerful arms tapered down to a flat stomach and lean hips. He had had a quick shower, evidently, and one of the cheap, white hand towels was slung around his neck and hung over his shoulders. She felt faint.

'I thought I'd get rid of the shirt as well,' he said. 'If you wouldn't mind laundering the lot, I would be extremely grateful. I failed to make provisions for clearing snow.'

Brianna blinked, as gauche and confused as a teenager. She saw that he was dangling the laundry bag on one finger while looking at her with amusement.

Well of course he would be, she thought, bristling. Writer or not, he came from a big city and, yes, was ever so patronising about the *smallness* of their town. And here she was, playing into his hands, gaping as though she had never seen a naked man in her life before, as though he was the most interesting thing to have landed on her doorstep in a hundred years.

'Well, perhaps you should have,' she said tartly. 'Only a fool would travel to this part of the world in the depths of winter and *not* come prepared for heavy snow.' She snatched the laundry bag from him and thrust the armful of clothes at his chest in return.

'Come again?' *Had she just called him a fool?*

'I haven't got the time or the energy to launder your clothes every two seconds because you didn't anticipate bad weather. In February. Here.' Her eyes skirted nervously away from the aggressive width of his chest. 'And I suggest,' she continued tightly, 'That you cover up. If I don't have the time to launder your clothes, then I most certainly do not have the time to play nursemaid when you go down with flu!'

Leo was trying to think of the last time a woman had raised her voice in his presence. Or, come to think of it, said anything that was in any way inflammatory. It just didn't happen. He didn't know whether to be irritated, enraged or entertained.

'Message understood loud and clear.' He grinned and leaned against the doorframe. However serious the implications of this visit to the land that time forgot, he realised that he was enjoying himself. Right now, at this very moment, with this beautiful Irish girl standing in front of him, glaring and uncomfortable. 'Fortunately, I'm as healthy as a horse. Can't remember the last time I succumbed to flu. So you won't have to pull out your nurse's uniform and tend to me.' Interesting notion, though… His dark eyes drifted over her lazily. 'I'll be down shortly. And my thanks once again for the clothes.'

Brianna was still hot and flustered when, half an hour later, he sauntered down to the kitchen. One of the tables in the bar area had been neatly set for one. 'I hope you're not expecting me to have lunch on my own,' were his opening words, and she spun around from where she had been frowning into the pot of homemade soup.

Without giving her a chance to answer, he began searching for the crockery, giving a little grunt of satisfaction when he hit upon the right cupboard. 'Remember we were going to…talk? You were going to tell me all about the people who live here so that I can get some useful fodder for my book.' It seemed inconceivable that a budding author would simply up sticks and go on a rambling tour of Ireland in the hope of inspiration but, as excuses went, it had served its purpose, which was all that mattered. 'And then, I'll do whatever you want me to do. I'm a man of my word.'

'There won't be much to do,' Brianna admitted. 'The snow's not letting up. I've phoned Aidan and told him that the place will be closed until the weather improves.'

'Aidan?'

'One of my friends. He can be relied on to spread the word. Only my absolute regulars would even contemplate trudging out here in this weather.'

'So…is Aidan the old would-be opera singer?'

'Aidan is my age. We used to go to school together.' She dished him out some soup, added some bread and offered him a glass of wine, which he rejected in favour of water.

'And he's the guy who broke your heart? No. He wouldn't be. The guy who broke your heart has long since disappeared, hasn't he?'

Brianna stiffened. She reminded herself that she was not having a cosy chat with a friend over lunch. This was a guest in her pub, a stranger who was passing through, no more. Confiding details of her private life was beyond the pale, quite different from chatting about all the amusing things that happened in a village where nearly everyone knew everyone else. Her personal life was not going to be fodder for a short story on life in a quaint Irish village.

'I don't recall telling you anything about my heart being broken, and I don't think my private life is any of your business. I hope the soup is satisfactory.'

So that was a sore topic; there was no point in a follow-up. It was irrelevant to his business here. If he happened to be curious, then it was simply because he was in the unique situation of being pub-bound and snowed in with just her for company. In the absence of anyone else, it was only natural that she would spark an interest.

'Why don't you serve food? It would add a lot to the profits of a place like this. You'd be surprised how remote places can become packed if the food is good enough...' He doubted the place had seen any changes in a very long time. Again, not his concern, he thought. 'So, if you don't want to talk about yourself, then that's fair enough.'

'Why don't *you* talk about yourself? Are you married? Do you have children?'

'If I were married and had children, I wouldn't be doing what I'm doing.' Marriage? Children? He had never contemplated either. He pushed the empty soup bowl aside and sprawled on the chair, angling it so that he could stretch his legs out to one side. 'Tell me about the old guy who likes to sing.'

'What made you suddenly decide to pack in your job and write? It must have been a big deal, giving up steady work in favour of a gamble that might or might not pay off.'

Leo shrugged and told himself that, certainly in this instance, the ends would more than justify the means—and at any rate, there was no chance that she would discover his little lie. He would forever remain the enigmatic stranger who had passed through and collected a few amusing anecdotes on the way. She would be regaling her friends with this in a week's time.

'Sometimes life is all about taking chances,' he murmured softly.

Brianna hadn't taken a chance in such a long time that she had forgotten what it felt like. The last chance she had taken had been with Danny, and hadn't *that* backfired spectacularly in her face? She had settled into a groove and had firmly convinced herself that it suited her. 'Some people are braver than others when it comes to that sort of thing,' she found herself muttering under her breath.

Leading remark, Leo thought. He had vast experience of women dangling titbits of information about themselves, offering them to him in the hope of securing his interest, an attempt to reel him in through his curiosity. However, for once his cynicism was absent. This woman knew nothing about him. He did not represent a rich, eligible bachelor. He was a struggling writer with no job. He had a glimpse of what it must feel like to communicate with a woman without undercurrents of suspicion that, whatever they wanted, at least part of it had to do with his limitless bank balance. He might have been adopted into a life of extreme privilege, and that privilege might have been his spring board to the dizzying heights of his success, but with that privilege and with that success had come drawbacks—one of which was an inborn mistrust of women and their motivations.

Right now, he was just communicating with a very beautiful and undeniably sexy woman and, hell, she was clueless about him. He smiled, enjoying the rare sense of freedom.

'And you're not one of the brave ones?'

Brianna stood up to clear the table. She had no idea where this sudden urge to confide was coming from. Was she bonding with him because, underneath those disconcerting good looks, he was a fellow artist? Because, on some weird level, he *understood* her? Or was she just one of those sad women, too young to be living a life of relative solitude, willing to confide in anyone who showed an interest?

Her head was buzzing. She felt hot and bothered and, when he reached out and circled her wrist with his hand, she froze in shock. The feel of his warm fingers on her skin was electrifying. She hadn't had a response like this to a man in a very long time. It was a feeling of coming alive. She wanted to snatch her hand away from his and rub away where he had touched her... Yet she also wanted him to keep his fingers on her wrist; she wanted to prolong the warm, physical connection between them. She abruptly sat back down, because her legs felt like jelly, and he released her.

'It's hard to take chances when you have commitments,' she muttered unsteadily. She couldn't tear her eyes away from his face. She literally felt as though he held her spellbound. 'You're on your own. You probably had sufficient money saved to just take off and do your own thing. I'm only now beginning to see the light financially and, even so, I still couldn't just up and leave.' She was leaning forward in the chair, leaning towards him as though he was the source of her energy. 'I should get this place tidied up,' she said agitatedly.

'Why? I thought you said that the pub would be closed until further notice.'

'Yes, but…'

'You must get lonely here on your own.'

'Of course I'm not lonely! I have too many friends to count!'

'But I don't suppose you have a lot of time to actually go out with them…'

Hot colour invaded her cheeks. No time to go out with them; no time even to pursue her art as a hobby. She hated the picture he was painting of her life. She was being made to feel as though she had sleepwalked into an existence of living from one day to the next, with each day being exactly the same. She dragged herself back to re-

ality, back to the fact that he was just a budding
writer on the hunt for some interesting material
for his book. He wasn't interested in *her*.

'Will I be the sad spinster in your book?' She
laughed shakily and gathered herself together. 'I
think you're better off with some of the more col-
ourful characters who live here.' She managed to
get to her feet, driven by a need to put some distance between them. How could she let this one
passing stranger get to her with such breath-tak-
ing speed? Lots of guys had come on to her over
the years. Some of them she had known for ever,
others had been friends of friends of friends. She
had laughed and joked with all of them but she
had never, not once, felt like *this*. Felt as though
the air was being sucked out of her lungs every
time she took a peek…as though she was being
injected with adrenaline every time she came
too close.

She busied herself tidying, urging him to sit
rather than help. Her flustered brain screeched
to a halt when she imagined them standing side
by side at the kitchen sink.

She launched into nervous conversation, chattering mindlessly about the last time a snow storm
had hit the village, forcing herself to relax as she
recounted stories of all the things that could happen to people who were snow bound for days
on end, occasionally as long as a fortnight: the

baby delivered by one panicked father; the rowdy rugby group who had been forced to spend two nights in the pub; the community spirit when they had all had to help each other out; the food that Seamus Riley had had to lift by rope into his bedroom because he hadn't been able to get past his front door.

Leo listened politely. He really ought to be paying a bit more attention, but he was captivated by the graceful movement of her tall, slender body as she moved from counter to counter, picking things up, putting things away, making sure not to look at him.

'In fact, we all do our bit when the weather turns really bad,' she was saying now as she turned briefly in his direction. 'I don't suppose you have much of that in London.'

'None,' Leo murmured absently. Her little breasts pointed against the jumper and he wondered whether she was wearing a bra; a sensible, white cotton bra. He never imagined the thought of a sensible, white cotton bra could be such an illicit turn-on.

He was so absorbed in the surprising disobedience of his imagination that he almost missed the name that briefly passed her lips and, when it registered, he stiffened and felt his pulses quicken.

'Sorry,' he grated, straightening. 'I missed that…particular anecdote.' He kept his voice as casual as possible but he was tense and vigilant as he waited for her to repeat what she had been saying, what he had stupidly missed because he had been too busy getting distracted, too busy missing the point of why he was stuck here in the first place.

'I was just telling you about what it's like here—we help each other out. I was telling you about my friend who lives in the village. Bridget McGuire…'

CHAPTER THREE

So HIS MOTHER wasn't the drunk or the junkie that he had anticipated, if his landlady was to be believed...

Leo flexed his muscles and wandered restlessly through the lounge where he had been sitting in front of his computer working for the past hour and a half.

Circumstance had forced him into a routine of sorts, as his optimistic plan of clearing off within a few days had faded into impossibility.

After three days, the snow was still falling steadily. It fluctuated between virtual white-out and gentle flakes that could lull you into thinking that it was all picture-postcard perfect. Until you opened the front door and clocked that the snow you'd cleared moments previously had already been replaced by a fresh fall.

He strolled towards the window and stared out at a pitch-black vista, illuminated only by the outside lights which Brianna kept on overnight.

It was not yet seven in the morning. He had

never needed much sleep and here, more than ever, he couldn't afford to lie in. Not when he had to keep communicating with his office, sending emails, reviewing reports, without her knowing exactly what was going on. At precisely seven-thirty, he would shut his computer and head outside to see what he could do about beating back some of the snow so that it didn't completely bank up against the door.

It was, he had to admit to himself, a fairly unique take on winter sport. When he had mentioned that to Brianna the day before, she had burst out laughing and told him that he could try building himself a sledge and having fun outside, getting in touch with his inner child.

He made himself a cup of coffee and reined in the temptation to let his mind meander, which was what it seemed to want to do whenever he thought of her.

His mother was in hospital recovering from a mild heart attack.

'She should have been out last week,' Brianna had confided, 'But they've decided to keep her in because the weather's so horrendous and she has no one to take care of her.'

Where was the down-and-out junkie he had been anticipating? Of course, there was every chance that she *had* been a deadbeat, a down and out. It would be a past she would have wanted to keep to herself, especially with Brianna who, from the sounds of it, saw her as something of a surrogate mother. The woman hadn't lived her whole life in the village. Who knew what sort of person she had been once upon a time?

But certainly, the stories he had heard did not tally with his expectations.

And the bottom line was that his hands were tied at the moment. He had come to see for himself what his past held. He wasn't about to abandon that quest on the say-so of a girl he'd known for five minutes. On the other hand, he was now on indefinite leave. One week, he had told his secretary, but who was to say that this enforced stay would not last longer?

The snow showed no sign of abating. When it *did* abate, there was still the question of engineering a meeting with his mother. She was in hospital and when she came out she would presumably be fairly weak. However, without anyone to act as full-time carer, at least for a while, what was the likelihood of her being released from hospital? He was now playing a waiting game.

And throughout all this, there was still the matter of his fictitious occupation. Surely Brianna would start asking him questions about this so-called book he was busily writing? Would he have to fabricate a plot?

In retrospect, out of all the occupations he

could have picked, he concluded that he had managed to hit on the single worst one of them all. God knew, he hadn't read a book in years. His reading was strictly of the utilitarian variety: legal tomes, books on the movements of financial markets, detailed backgrounds to companies he was planning to take over.

The fairly straightforward agenda he had set out for himself was turning into something far more complex.

He turned round at the sound of her footsteps on the wooden floor.

And that, he thought, frowning, was an added complication. She was beginning to occupy far too much space in his head. Familiarity was not breeding contempt. He caught himself watching her, thinking about her, fantasising about her. His appreciation of her natural beauty was growing like an unrestrained weed, stifling the disciplined part of his brain that told him that he should not go there.

Not only was she ignorant of his real identity but whatever the hell had happened to her— whoever had broken her heart, the mystery guy she could not be persuaded to discuss—had left her vulnerable. On the surface, she was capable, feisty, strong-willed and stubbornly proud. But he sensed her vulnerability underneath and the rational part of him acknowledged that a vulnerable woman was a woman best left well alone.

But his libido was refusing to listen to reason and seemed to have developed a will of its own.

'You're working too hard.' She greeted him cheerfully. Having told him that she would not be doing his laundry, she had been doing his laundry. Today he was wearing the jeans she had washed the day before and one of her father's checked flannel shirts, the sleeves of which he had rolled to the elbows. In a few seconds, she took in the dark hair just visible where the top couple of buttons of the shirt were undone; the low-slung jeans that emphasised the leanness of his hips; the strong, muscular forearms.

Leo knew what he had been working on and it hadn't been the novel she imagined: legal technicalities that had to be sorted out with one small IT company he was in the process of buying; emails to the human resources department so that they reached a mutually agreeable deal with employees of yet another company he was acquiring. He had the grace to flush.

'Believe me, I've worked harder,' he said with utmost truth. She was in some baggy grey jogging bottoms, which made her look even slimmer than she was, and a baggy grey sweatshirt. For the first time, her hair wasn't tied back, but instead fell over her shoulders and down her back in a cascade of rich auburn.

'I guess maybe in that company of yours—'

'Company of mine?' Leo asked sharply and then realised that guilt had laced the question with unnecessary asperity when she smiled and explained that she was talking about whatever big firm he had worked for before quitting.

She had noticed that he never talked about the job he had done, and Brianna had made sure to steer clear of the subject. It was a big enough deal getting away from the rat race without being reminded of what you'd left behind, because the rat race from which he had escaped was the very same rat race that was now funding his exploits into the world of writing.

'You still haven't told me much about your book,' she said tentatively. 'I know I'm being horribly nosy, and I know how hard it is to let someone have a whiff of what you're working on before it's finished, but you must be very far in. You start work so early and I know you keep it up, off and on during the day. You never seem to lack inspiration.'

Leo considered what level of inspiration was needed to review due diligence on a company: none. 'You know how it goes,' he said vaguely. 'You can write two…er…chapters and then immediately delete them, although…' He considered the massive deal he had just signed off on. 'I must admit I've been reasonably productive. To change the subject, have you any books I could borrow? I had no idea I would be in one place for so long…'

When had his life become so blinkered? he wondered. Sure, he played; he enjoyed the company of beautiful women, but they were a secondary consideration to his work. The notion of any of them becoming a permanent fixture in his life had never crossed his mind. And, yes, he relaxed at the gym but, hell, he hadn't picked up a novel in years; hadn't been to a movie in years; rarely watched television for pleasure, aside from the occasional football match; went to the theatre occasionally, usually when it was an arranged company event, but even then he was always restless, always thinking of what needed to be done with his companies or clients or mergers or buyouts.

He impatiently swept aside the downward spiral of introspection and surfaced to find her telling him that there were books in her study.

'And there's something I want to show you,' she said hesitantly. She disappeared for a few minutes and in that time he strolled around the lounge, distractedly looking at the fire and wondering whether the log basket would have to be topped up. He wondered how much money she was losing with this enforced closure of the pub and then debated the pros and cons of asking her if he could have a look at her books.

'Okay…'

Leo turned around and walked slowly towards her. 'What do you have behind your back?'

Brianna took a deep breath and revealed one of the small paintings she had done a few months back, when she had managed to squeeze in some down-time during the summer. It was a painting of the lake and in the foreground an angler sat, back to the spectator, his head bent, his body leaning forward, as if listening for the sound of fish.

'I don't like showing my work to anyone either,' she confided as he took the picture from her and held it at a distance in his hands. 'So I fully understand why you don't want to talk about your book.'

'*You* painted this?'

'What do you think?'

'I think you're wasted running a pub here.' Leo was temporarily lost for words. Of course he had masterpieces in his house, as well as some very expensive investment art, but this was charming and unique enough to find a lucrative market of its own. 'Why don't you try selling them?'

'Oh, I could never produce enough.' She sighed regretfully. She moved to stand next to him so that they were both looking at the painting. When he rested it on the table, she didn't move, and suddenly her throat constricted as their eyes tangled and, for a few seconds, she found that she was holding her breath.

Leo sifted his fingers through her hair and the door slammed shut on all his good intentions not to let his wayward libido do the thinking for him. He just knew that he wanted this woman, more than he had ever wanted any woman in his life before, and for the hell of him he had no idea why. He had stopped trying to work that one out. He was not a man who was accustomed to holding out. Desire was always accompanied by possession. In fact, as he looked down at her flushed, upturned face, he marvelled that he had managed to restrain himself for so long because hadn't he known, almost from the very start, that she was attracted to him? Hadn't he seen it there in those hot, stolen looks and her nervous, jumpy reactions when he got fractionally too close to her?

He perched on the edge of the table and drew her closer to him.

Brianna released her breath in a long shudder. She was burning up where he touched her. Never in a million years would she have imagined that she could do this, that she could *feel* this way, feel so connected to a guy that she wanted him to touch her after only a few days. Showing him that painting, had he only known it, had been a measure of how much she trusted him. She felt *easy* in his company. Gone were the feelings of suspicion which had been there when she had first laid eyes on him, when she had wondered what such a dramatic looking stranger was doing in their midst, standing there at the door of the pub and looking around him with guarded coolness.

She had let down her defences, had thawed. Being cooped up had blurred the lines between paying guest and a guy who was as amusing as he was intelligent; as witty and dry as he was focused and disciplined. He might have worked in a company and done boring stuff but you would never guess that by the breadth of his conversation. He knew a great deal about art, about world affairs, and he had travelled extensively. He had vaguely told her that it was all in connection with his job, and really not very exciting at all because he did nothing but work when he got to his destination, but he could still captivate her with descriptions of the places he had been and the things he had seen there.

In short, he was nothing at all like any of the men she had ever met in her entire life, and that included Danny Fluke.

'What are you doing?' she asked weakly.

'I'm touching you. Do you want me to stop?'

'This is crazy.'

'This is taking a chance.'

'I don't even...know you.'

No, she certainly didn't. And yet, strangely, she knew more about him than any other woman did. Not that there was any point in getting tied down with semantics. 'What does that have to do with wanting someone?' His voice was a low murmur in her ear and, as he slid his hand underneath the jumper to caress her waist, she could feel all rational thought disappearing like dew in the summer sun.

So, she thought, fighting down the temptation to moan as his fingers continued to stroke her bare skin, he wasn't going to be sticking around. He was as nomadic as she was rooted to this place. But wasn't that what taking chances was all about?

She reached up and trembled as she linked her fingers behind his neck and pulled him down towards her.

His kiss was soft, exploratory. His tongue mingled against hers and was mind-blowingly erotic. He angled his long legs open and she edged her body between them so that now she was pushed up against him and could feel the hardness of his erection against her.

'You can still tell me to stop...' And, if she did, he didn't know what he would do. Have a sub-zero shower? Even then, he wasn't sure that it would be enough to cool him down. 'Taking a chance can sometimes be a dangerous indulgence...'

And yet there was a part of her that knew that *not* taking this chance would be a source of eternal regret. Besides, why on earth should she let one miserable experience that was now in the past determine her present?

'Maybe I want to live dangerously for once...'

His hand had crept further up her jumper and he unhooked her bra strap with practised ease.

Brianna's breath caught in her throat and she stilled as he inched his way towards one small breast. She quivered at the feel of his thumb rubbing over it. She wanted him so badly that she was shaking with desire.

Leo marvelled that something he knew they just shouldn't be doing could feel so damned *right*. Had he been going stir crazy here without even realising it? Was that why he had been so useless at disciplining his libido? The lie that had taken him so far, that had started life as just something he had been inspired to do because he had needed an excuse for being there in the first place, hung around his neck with the deadly weight of an albatross.

He shied away from the thought that she might find out, and then laughed at the possibility of that happening.

'I won't be around for much longer.' He felt

compelled to warn her off involvement even though he knew that the safest route he could take if he really didn't want to court unwanted involvement would be to walk away. 'Sure you want to take a chance with someone who's just passing through?' He spoke against her mouth and he could feel her warm breath mingling with his.

Brianna feverishly thought of the last guy she had become involved with—the guy she had thought wasn't passing through, the guy she had thought she might end up spending the rest of her life with but who, in fact, had always known that he would be moving on. This time, there would be no illusions. A fling: it was something she had never done in her life before. Danny had been her first and only relationship.

'I'm not looking for permanence,' she whispered. 'I thought I had that once and it turned out to be the biggest mistake I ever made. Stop talking.'

'Happy to oblige,' Leo growled, his conscience relieved. 'I think I wanted this within hours of meeting you.' He circled her waist with his hands and then pushed the jumper up, taking the bra with it as well.

For a split second, Brianna was overwhelmed by shyness. She closed her eyes and arched back, every nerve and pore straining towards a closeness she hadn't felt in such a long time. When she felt the wetness of his mouth surround her nipple, she groaned and half-collapsed. Her hands coiled into his thick, dark hair as he continued sucking and teasing the stiffened peaks until she wanted to faint from the pleasure of it. When he drew back, she groaned in frustration and looked at him drowsily from under her lashes, her heart-beat quickening to a frantic beat as she watched him inspecting her breasts with the same con-sidered thoroughness with which he had earlier inspected her painting.

'I want to see you,' Leo said roughly. He was surprised at the speed with which his body was reacting, racing towards release. His erection was uncomfortable against his jeans, bulging pain-fully. Yet he didn't want to rush this. He had to close his eyes briefly and breathe deeply so that he wouldn't be thrown off-balance by the sight of her bare breasts, small and crested with large, pink nipples that were still glistening from where he had sucked them.

In response, Brianna traced the contours of his shoulders, broad and powerful. It was driving her crazy just thinking about touching his chest, the bronzed, muscled chest that had sent her imagi-nation into overdrive on that first day when he had stood half-naked in front of her, waiting for the shirts she had brought for him.

'I don't want to make love to you here...' He swung her off her feet as though she weighed nothing and carried her up the stairs towards his bedroom, and then, pausing briefly, up the further flight of stairs that led to her bedroom. He didn't dare look down at her soft, small breasts or he would deposit her on the stairs and take her right there. His urgency to have her lying underneath him was shocking. Not cool; definitely not his style.

He found her bedroom, barely taking time to look around him as he placed her on the bed and ordered her to stay put.

'Where do you think I'm going to go?' She laughed with nervous excitement and levered herself onto one elbow, watching with unconcealed fascination as he began to strip off. With each discarded item of clothing, her heart rate picked up speed until she had to close her eyes and take deep breaths.

Her response was so wonderfully, naturally open and unconcealed that Leo experienced a raw, primitive thrill that magnified his burning lust a thousand-fold.

He took his time removing the jeans because he was enjoying watching her watching him. Most of all he enjoyed her gasp as he stepped out of his boxers and moved towards her, his erection thick, heavy and impressively telling of just how aroused he was.

Brianna scrabbled to sit up, pulses racing, the blood pumping in her veins hot with desire.

She couldn't believe she was doing this, behaving in a way that was so out of character. She sighed and moaned as the mattress depressed under his weight; the feel of his hands tucking into the waistband of the jogging bottoms, sliding them down, signalled the final nail in her crumbling defences

'You're beautiful.' He straddled her and kissed her with intimate, exquisite thoroughness, tracing her mouth with his tongue, then trailing his lips against her neck so that she whimpered and tilted her head to prolong the kiss.

Every small noise she made, every tiny movement, bore witness to how much she was turned on and it gave him an unbelievable kick to know that she had allowed herself to be pulled along by an irresistible force even though it went against the grain.

Her skin was supple and smooth, her breasts perfect, dainty orbs that barely fitted his large hand.

He teased the tip of her nipple with his tongue and then submerged himself in the pleasure of suckling on it, loving the way she writhed under him; the way her fingers bit into his shoulder blades; the way she arched back, eyes closed, mouth parted, her whole body trembling.

He let his hand drift over her flat stomach to circle the indentation of her belly button with one finger while he continued to plunder her breasts, moving between them, sucking, liking the way he could draw them into his mouth. He was hungry for more but determined not to take things fast. He wanted to savour every second of tasting her body.

He parted her legs gently with his hand and eased the momentary tension he could feel as she stilled against him.

'Shh,' he whispered huskily, as though she had spoken. 'Relax.'

'It's…been a long time.' Brianna gave a half-stifled, nervous laugh. He raised his head and their eyes tangled, black clashing with apple-green.

'When you say *long*...'

'I haven't slept with anyone since… Well, it's been years…' She twisted away, embarrassed by the admission. Where had the time gone? It seemed as though one minute she had been nursing heartbreak, dealing with her father's death, caught up in a jumble of financial worries, her life thrown utterly off course, and the next minute she was here, still running the pub, though with the financial worries more or less behind her. She was hardly sinking but definitely not swimming and living a life that seemed far too responsible for someone her age.

Leo tilted her face to his, kissed her on the side of her mouth and banked down his momentary discomfort at thinking that he might be taking advantage of her.

Yet she was perfectly aware of the situation, perfectly aware that he wasn't going to be hanging around. Naturally, she was not in possession of the true facts regulating his departure, but weren't those just details? Looking at the bigger picture, she knew where she stood, that this was just a fling—not even that.

'I'll be gentle.'

'I guess you…you've had a lot of girlfriends?'

'I haven't espoused a life of celibacy.' He slipped his finger into the wet groove of her femininity and felt whatever further questions she wanted to ask become stifled under her heated response. She moved against his finger and groaned.

He could have played with her body all day, all night. Right now, he couldn't get enough of her and he moved downwards. She sucked in her breath sharply and he rested the palm of his hand flat on her stomach, then he nuzzled the soft hair covering the apex between her thighs. He breathed in the musky, honeyed scent of her and dipped his tongue to taste her. How did he know that this was something she was experiencing for the first time? And why was that such a turn on?

He teased the throbbing bud of her clitoris and, when she moaned and squirmed, he flattened his hands on her thighs so that her legs were spread wide open for his delectation.

Brianna had never known anything like this before. There wasn't a single part of her body that wasn't consumed with an overpowering craving. She wanted him to continue doing what he was doing, yet she wanted him in her, deep inside. She weakly tugged at his hair but was powerless to pull him up. When she looked down and saw his dark head between her legs, and his strong, bronzed hands against the paleness of her thighs, she almost passed out.

Could years of living in icy isolation have made her so vulnerable to his touch? Had her body been so deprived of human contact that it was now overwhelmed? It felt like it.

When he rose, she was so close to tipping over the edge that she had to squeeze her eyes shut and grit her teeth together to maintain self-control.

'Enjoying yourself?' Leo raised some hair from her flushed face to whisper in her ear. He rubbed his stiff erection against her belly and felt sensation lick through his body at frightening speed.

Brianna blushed and nodded, then raised her-self up so that she could kiss him on the mouth, draw him down over her so that their bodies were pressed together, fused with slick perspiration. She reached down and took him in her hand and he angled himself slightly away to accommodate her. His breathing thickened as she continued to work her movements into a deep rhythm.

He was impressively big and she shivered with heady anticipation.

'A condom… Wait; in my wallet…'

Already he was groping in the pocket of his jeans for his wallet and fumbling to fetch a con-dom, his eyes still pinned to her flushed, reclin-ing body. How on earth could he be thinking of *anything* at a time like this? She just couldn't wait for him to be inside her, filling her with his bigness.

'You're well prepared.' She sighed and thought that of course he would be; he was a man of the world after all.

She groaned and felt the slippery, cool sheath guarding his arousal; her hands impatiently guided him to her, longing for the moment when he would fill her completely. She flipped onto him and arched up, her hands on his broad chest, her small breasts tipping teasingly towards him. 'I know you're moving on and I like it that way.' Did she? Yes, she did! 'I *need* this.' She leaned forward, bottom sticking up provocatively, and covered her mouth with his. 'The last thing I would take a gamble on is with a pregnancy.'

'You wouldn't want to be stuck with a loser like me?' Leo grinned, because those words had never passed his lips before. 'A travelling writer hoping to make his fortune?' He curved his hands on her rear and inserted himself into her. He drove into her and Brianna felt a surge of splintering pleasure as he moved deep inside her. Her head was flung back and he could feel the ends of her long hair on his thighs, brushing against them.

'A guy could feel insulted.'

She was on her back before she knew it and he was rearing up over her, big, powerful and oh, so breathtakingly beautiful, one-hundred per cent alpha male.

She came with such intensity that she had to squeeze her eyes shut on the gathering tears. She knew her fingers were digging in to the small of his back and they dug harder as she felt him swell and reach his orgasm inside her.

God, nothing had ever felt *that* good. Years of celibacy, running the pub and coping with all the day-to-day worries had obviously had the effect of making her respond like a wanton to being touched. She had never been like that before. But then, she had been so much younger when she had met Danny. Had the years and the tough times released some sort of pent-up capacity for passion that she had never known about?

'So…' Leo drawled, rolling onto his side then pulling her to face him so that their naked bodies were front to front and still touching, almost as though neither of them wanted to break the physical contact. 'You were telling me all about how you were using me to get you out of a dry patch.' He inserted his thigh between her legs and felt her wetness slippery against his skin.

'I never said that,' Brianna murmured.

'You didn't have to. The word "need" gave it away.'

'Maybe you're right. It's been a slog for the past few years. Don't get me wrong, there have been times when I've enjoyed running this place. It's just not how I expected my life to turn out.'

'What had you expected?'

'I expected to be married with a couple of kids, pursuing the art career that never took off, as it happens.'

'Ah. And the couple of kids and the wedding ring would have been courtesy of the heartbreaker?'

'He dumped me.' It had haunted her, had been responsible for all the precautions she had taken to protect herself. Yet lying here, with his thigh doing wonderful things between her legs, stirring up all the excitement that had only just faded, she could barely remember Danny's face. He had stopped being a human being and had become just a vague, disturbing recollection of a past mistake. She couldn't care less what had become of him, so how on earth had he carried on having such an influence on her behaviour?

'I wasn't good enough,' she said, anger replacing the humiliation that usually accompanied this thought. 'We went out for ages; when I thought that we really were destined to be together, he broke it to me that I had just been a good time at university. Dad was ill and I had discovered that the guy I thought I was in love with had been using me all along for a bit of fun. At least *you've* been honest and up-front.'

'Honest and up-front?'

'You're moving on. You're not here to stay. No illusions. I like that.'

'Before you start putting me on a pedestal and getting out the feather brush to dust my halo, I should tell you that you know very little about me.'

'I know enough.'

'You have little to compare me with. I'm a pretty ruthless bastard, if you want the truth.'

Brianna laughed, a clear, tinkling sound of pure amusement. She sifted her fingers through his dark hair and curled up closer to him which kick-started a whole lot of very pleasurable sensations that had him hardening in record time.

He edged her back from him and looked at her, unsmiling. 'You've been hurt once. You've spent years buried here, working beyond the call of duty to keep the wolves from the door. You've had no boyfriends, no distractions to occupy your time. Hell, you haven't even been able to wring out an hour or two to do your painting. And then along I come. I'm not your knight in shining armour.'

'I never said that you were!' Brianna pulled back, hurt and confused at a sudden glimpse of ruthlessness she wouldn't have imagined possible.

'It's been my experience that what women say is often at variance to what they think. I won't be hanging around—and even if I lived next door to you, Brianna, I don't do long-term relationships.'

'What do you mean, you *don't do long-term relationships*?'

'Just what I say, so be warned. Don't make the mistake of investing anything in me. What we have is sexual attraction, pure and simple.' He softened and gentled his voice. 'We have something that works at this precise moment in time.'

But it was more than that. What about the conversations they had had; the moments of sharing generated by close proximity? Some sixth sense stopped her from pointing that out. She was finding it difficult to recognise the cool, dark eyes of this stranger looking at her.

'And stop treating me as though I'm a stupid kid,' she bit out tightly, disentangling herself from him. 'I was one of those once.' Her voice was equally cool. 'I don't intend to repeat the same mistake twice. And, if you think that I would ever let myself get emotionally wrapped up with someone who doesn't want to spend his life in one place, then you're crazy. I value security. When I fall for someone, it will be someone who wants to settle down and isn't scared of commitment. I'm thankful that you've been honest enough to tell me as it is, but you have nothing to fear. Your precious independence isn't at risk.'

'If that's the case, why are you pulling away from me?'

'I don't like your tone of voice.'

'Just so long as it's not what I say but how I'm saying it,' he murmured softly. He tugged her back towards him and Brianna placed her hand on his shoulder but it was a pathetically weak attempt to stave off the fierce urgings of her body.

As his hand swept erotically along her thigh, she shimmied back towards him, the coolness in his eyes forgotten, the jarring hardness of his voice consigned to oblivion.

They made love slowly, touching each other

everywhere, absorbing each other's pleasurable groans. She tasted him with as much hunger as he tasted her. She just couldn't get enough of him—at her breasts, between her thighs, urging her to tell him what she wanted him to do and telling her in explicit detail what he wanted her to do to him.

Eventually, just as she was falling into a light, utterly contented doze, she heard the insistent buzz of her mobile phone next to the bed where she had left it charging. She was almost too sleepy to pick up but, when she did, she instantly sat up, drawing the covers around her.

Leo watched her, his keen antennae picking up her sudden tension, although from this end of the phone he could only hear monosyllabic replies to whatever was being said.

'Remember I told you about my friend? Bridget McGuire?' Brianna ended the call thoughtfully but remained holding the mobile, caressing it absently.

Leo was immediately on red-hot alert, although he kept his expression mildly interested and utterly expressionless. 'The name rings a bell...'

'They need to release her from hospital. There's been an accident on the motorway and they need all the beds they can get. So she's leaving tomorrow. The snow is predicted to stop. She's coming here...'

CHAPTER FOUR

'WHEN?' HE SLID out of the bed, strolled towards the window and stared down to a snowy, grey landscape. The sun had barely risen but, yes, the snow appeared to be lessening.

This was the reason he was here, pretending to be someone he wasn't. When he had first arrived, he had wondered how a meeting with his mother could possibly be engineered in a town where everyone seemed to know everyone else. Several lies down and his quarry would be delivered right to his doorstep. Didn't fate work in mysterious ways?

Brianna, sitting up, wondered what was going through his head.

'For the moment, they're going to transfer her to another ward and then, provided the snow doesn't get worse, they're going to bring her here tomorrow. You're making me nervous, standing by the window like that. What are you thinking? I have room here at the pub. It won't make any difference to you. You won't have to vacate your room—in fact, you probably won't even notice that she's here. I shall have her in the spare room next to my bedroom so that I can keep a constant eye on her, and of course I doubt she'll be able to climb up and down stairs.'

Leo smiled and pushed himself away from the window ledge. When he tried to analyse what he felt about his birth mother, the most he could come up with was a scathing contempt which he realised he would have to attempt to conceal for what remained of his time here. Brianna might have painted a different picture, but years of pre-conceived notions were impossible to put to bed.

'So…' He slipped back under the covers and pulled her towards him. 'If we're going to have an unexpected visitor, then maybe you should start telling me the sort of person I can look forward to meeting and throw me a few more details…'

Brianna began plating their breakfast. Was it her imagination or was he abnormally interested in finding out about Bridget? He had returned to the bed earlier and she had thrown him a few sketchy details about her friend yet, off and on, he seemed to return to the subject. His questions were in no way pressing; in fact, he barely seemed to care about the answer.

A sudden thought occurred to her.

Was he really worried that their wonderful

one-on-one time might be interrupted? He had made it perfectly clear that he was just passing through, and had given her a stern warning that she was not to make the mistake of investing in him, yet was he becoming possessive of her company without even realising it himself?

For reasons best known to himself, he was a commitment-phobe, but did he respond out of habit? Had he warned her off because distancing himself was an automatic response?

He might not want to admit it, but over the past few days they had got to know one another in a way she would never have thought possible. He worked while she busied herself with the accounts and the bookkeeping but, for a lot of the time, they had communicated. He had even looked at her ledgers, leading her to think that he might have been an accountant in a previous life. He had suggested ways to improve her finances. He had persuaded her to show him all the paintings she had ever done, which she kept in portfolios under the bed, and had urged her to design a website to showcase them. She had caught herself telling him so much more than she had ever told anyone in her life before, even her close friends. He made a very good listener.

His own life, he had confided, had been as uneventful as it came: middle class, middle of the road. Both of them were single children, both

without parents. They laughed at the same things;
they bickered over the remote control for the television in the little private lounge which was set
aside for the guests, on those rare occasions she
had some. With the pub closed, they had had
lots of quality time during which to get to know
one another.

So was he *scared* that the arrival of Bridget
would signal the end of what they had?

With a sigh, she acknowledged that if the ambulance could make it up the lane to the pub to
deliver their patient then her loyal customers
could certainly make it as well. The pub would
once again reopen and their time together would
certainly be curtailed.

'I've been thinking,' she said slowly, handing
him a plate of bacon, eggs and toast and sitting
down. 'I might just keep the pub closed for a couple of weeks. Until the snow is well and truly over
and the path outside the pub is completely safe.'

She told herself that this was something that
made perfect sense. And why shouldn't she have
a little break? The last break she had had was
over summer when she had grabbed a long weekend to go to Dublin with her friends. At other
times, while they'd been off having lovely warm
holidays in sunny Spain or Portugal, she had always been holed up at the pub, unable to take

the time off because she couldn't afford to lose the revenue.

So why shouldn't she have time off now? A couple of weeks wouldn't break the bank—at least, not completely. And she would make up for it later in the year. Leo had suggested a website to promote the pub and she would take him up on that. He had intimated that she could really take off with only minimal changes, a few things to bring the place up to date.

And, if she closed the pub for a couple of weeks, they would continue to have their quality time until he disappeared.

'It would be better for Bridget as well,' she hurried on, not wanting to analyse how much of this idea was down to her desire to keep him to herself for a little longer. 'She's going to need looking after, at least in the beginning, and it would give me the opportunity to really take care of her without having to worry about running the pub as well.'

'Makes sense, I suppose...'

'You won't be affected at all.'

'I know. You've already told me.'

'And I don't want you to think that your needs are going to be overlooked. I mean, what I'm trying to say is...'

Leo tilted his head to one side. She blushed very easily. Especially when you considered the hard life she had had and the financial worries she had faced. No one would ever be able to accuse her of not being a fighter.

'Is that you'll carry on making my breakfast for me? Fixing me sandwiches for lunch? Slaving over a recipe book for something to cook for dinner? Making sure my bed is…warm and that you're in it?'

'I'm not part of a package deal.' Brianna bristled, suddenly offended at the picture he painted of her. 'You haven't paid for me along with the breakfast, lunch and dinner.' She stood up and began clearing the dishes, only pausing when she felt his arms around her at the sink. When she looked straight ahead, she could see their dim reflection in the window pane, his head downbent, buried in her hair. He didn't like it when she tied it back so she had left it loose the past couple of days and now he wound one of the long, auburn strands around his finger.

His other hand reached underneath the sweater and she watched their hazy reflection, the movement of his hand caressing her breast, playing with her nipple, rubbing the pad of his thumb over it. Liquid pooled between her legs, dampening her underwear and making her squirm and shift in his embrace.

She could feel his hard arousal nudging her from behind and, when she half-closed her eyes, her imagination took flight, dwelling on the image of her touching him there, licking and sucking with his fingers tangled in her hair. She wanted to do the same now. She pictured him kneeling like a penitent at her feet, her body pressing against the wall in her bedroom, her legs parted as he tasted her.

He seemed to have the ability to make her stop thinking the second he laid a finger on her and he did it as easily as someone switching a tap off.

She watched, eyes smoky with desire, as he pushed the jumper up; now she could see the pale skin of her stomach and his much darker hands on her breasts, massaging them, teasing them, playing with her swollen, sensitive nipples.

She shuddered and angled her neck so that he could kiss her.

'I know you're not part of the package,' he murmured. 'And, just to set the record straight, I enjoy you a hell of a lot more than I enjoy the meals you prepare.'

'Are you implying that I'm a bad cook?' He had undone the top button of her jeans and she wriggled as he did the same with the zip, easing the jeans down over her slim hips, exposing her pale pink briefs.

'You're a fantastic cook. One of the best.' He stood back slightly so that she could swivel to face him.

'You're a terrible liar.'

Leo flushed guiltily at this unwittingly inaccurate swipe, said in jest.

'Don't bank on that,' he murmured into her ear. 'You forget that I've already warned you that I'm a ruthless bastard.'

'If you really *were* a ruthless bastard, then you wouldn't have to warn me. I'd see all the giveaway signs.' She tiptoed and drew his head down so that she could kiss him. Her body was heating up, impatiently anticipating the moment when it could unite with his.

In the heat of passion, it was always him who thought about protection. So he was scrupulous when it came to taking no chances—that didn't mean that he wasn't becoming more attached to her, did it? The fact he didn't want an unwanted pregnancy any more than she did, didn't indicate that his nomadic lifestyle wasn't undergoing a subtle ground-change...

'Touch me,' he commanded roughly and he rested his hands on her hips and half-closed his eyes as she burrowed underneath his jumper, her hands feathering across his chest, pausing to do wonderful things to his nipples. He was breathing quickly, every sinew and muscle stretched to a point of yearning that made a nonsense of his legendary self-control.

He yanked his jumper off and heard her sigh

with pleasure, a little, soft sigh that was uniquely hers. His eyes were still half-closed and he inhaled slightly to accommodate her fumbling fingers as they travelled downwards to unbutton and unzip his jeans.

Outside a watery sun was making itself known, pushing through the blanket of leaden grey of the past few days. Like an unfamiliar visitor, it threaded its way tentatively into the kitchen, picking up the rich hues of her hair and the smooth, creamy whiteness of her skin.

He stilled as she lowered herself to begin pulling down his jeans, taking his boxers with them until they were at his ankles and he stepped out of them and kicked them to one side.

He couldn't withhold his grunt of intense satisfaction as she began delicately to lick the tip of his erection. He was so aroused that it was painful and as he looked down at the crown of her head, and her pink, darting tongue as it continued to tease him, he became even more aroused.

'You're driving me crazy, woman...' His voice was unsteady, as were his hands as he coiled his fingers into her hair.

Brianna didn't say anything. His nakedness had her firing on all cylinders and his vulnerability, glimpses of which she only caught when they were making love, was the most powerful of aphrodisiacs. She took him in her mouth, loving the way every atom of pleasure seemed to be transmitted from him to her via invisible, powerful pathways. As she sucked and teased, her hands caressed, and she was aware of his big, strong body shaking ever so slightly. How could he make her feel so powerful and so helpless at the same time?

She was so damp, her body so urgent for his, that she itched to rip off her clothes. Her jumper was back in place and it felt heavy and uncomfortable against her sensitised skin. She gasped as he pulled her up, and she obediently lifted her arms so that he could remove the offending jumper. The cool air hit her heated breasts like a soothing balm.

'I can't make it to the bedroom…' He breathed heavily as she wriggled out of the jeans and then he hoisted her onto the kitchen table, shoving aside the remnants of their breakfast—the jar of marmalade, the little ceramic butter dish, the striped jug with milk. Surprisingly, nothing crashed to the ground in the process.

When he stood back, he marvelled at the sight of her naked beauty: her arms outstretched, her eyes heavy with the same lust that was coursing through his bloodstream like an unstoppable virus.

Her vibrant hair streamed out around her, formed a tangle over one breast, and the glimpse of a pink nipple peeping out was like something from an erotic X-rated magazine. Her parted legs were an invitation he couldn't refuse, nor was his body allowing him the luxury of foreplay. As she raised her knees, he embedded himself into her in one hard, forceful thrust and then he lifted her up and drove again into her, building a furious rhythm and somehow ending up with her pressed against the kitchen wall, her legs wrapped around him.

Her hair trailed over her shoulder, down her back, a silky mass of rich auburn. He felt her in every part of him in a way that had never happened with any woman before. He didn't get it, but he liked it. He was holding her underneath her sexy, rounded bottom and as he thrust long and deep into her he looked down at her little breasts bouncing in time to their bodies. The tips of her nipples were stiff and swollen, the big, flattened pink discs encircling them swollen and puffy. Every square inch of her body was an unbelievable turn-on and, even as he felt the satiny tightness of her sheath around him, he would have liked to close his mouth over one of those succulent nipples so that he could feast on its honeyed sweetness.

They came as one, their bodies fused, their breathing mirroring each other.

'That was…indescribable.' He eased her down

and they stood facing one another, completely naked. Sanity began restoring itself, seeping through the haze of his hot, replete satisfaction. He swore under his breath and turned away. 'The condom…it seems to have split…'

Brianna's eyes widened with shock. She went over to her bundle of clothes and began getting dressed. He looked horrified. There was a heavy, laden silence as he likewise began getting dressed.

'It's okay. It takes more than one mistake for a person to get pregnant! If you read any magazine there are always stories of women trying for months, *years,* to conceive…' Her menstrual cycle had always been erratic so it was easy to believe that.

Leo shook his head and raked his fingers through his hair. 'This is a nightmare.'

'I won't get pregnant! I'm one-hundred per cent sure about that! I know my body. You don't have to look as though…as though the sky has fallen in!'

Yes, he was a nomad. Yes, he had just jacked in his job to embark on a precarious and unpredictable career. But did he have to look so damned *appalled*? And then, hard on the heels of that thought, came wrenching dismay at the insanity of thinking that a pregnancy wouldn't be the end of the world. God, what was she *thinking*? Had she gone completely *mad*?

She snatched the various bits and pieces left on the kitchen table and began slamming them into cupboards.

'God knows, you're probably right,' he gritted, catching her by the arm and pulling her round to face him. 'But I've had sufficient experience of the fairer sex to know that they—'

'*What* experience? What are you talking about?'

Leo paused. Money bred suspicion and he had always been suspicious enough to know that it was a mistake to trust contraception to the opposite sex.

Except, how could he say that when he was supposed to be a struggling writer existing on the remnants of his savings from whatever two-bit job he had been in? How could he confess that five years previously he had had a scare with a woman in the dying stages of their relationship. The Pill she claimed to have been on, which she then later denied... Two weeks of hell cursing himself for having been a trusting idiot and, in the end, thankfully there had been no pregnancy. There was nothing he could have done in the circumstances, but a split condom was still bad news.

But how could he concede that his vast financial reserves made him a natural target for potential gold- diggers?

'You must really think that you're such a desirable catch that women just can't help wanting to tie you down by falling pregnant!'

'So you're telling me that I'm *not* a desirable catch?' Crisis over. Deception, even as an acceptable means to an end, was proving unsavoury. He smiled a sexy half-smile, clearing his head of any shade of guilt, telling himself that a chance in a million did not constitute anything to get worked up about.

'There are better options…' The tension slowly seeped out of her although she was tempted to pry further, to find out who these determined women were—the ones he had bedded, the ones who had wanted more.

She tried to picture him in his other life, sitting in a cubicle behind a desk somewhere with a computer in front of him. She couldn't. He seemed so at home in casual clothes; dealing with the snow; making sure the fireplace was well supplied with logs; doing little handyman jobs around the place, the sort she usually ended up having to pay someone to do for her. He now had a stubbly six o'clock shadow on his jawline because he told her that he saw no point in shaving twice a day. He was a man made for the great outdoor life. And yet…

'You were going to tell me about Bridget,' Leo said casually, moving to sit at the table and shoving his chair out so that he could stretch his legs in front of him. 'Before you rudely decided to interrupt the conversation by demanding sex.'

Brianna laughed. Just like that, whatever mood had swept over her like an ugly, freak wave looming unexpectedly from calm waters dissolved and disappeared.

'As I said, you'll like her.' She began unloading the dishwasher, her mind only half-focused on what she was saying; she was looking ahead to the technicalities of keeping the pub shut, wondering how long she could afford the luxury, trying to figure out whether her battered four-wheel drive could make it to the village so that she could stock up on food…

Leo's lips twisted with disdain. 'Funnily enough, whenever someone has said that to me in the past I'm guaranteed to dislike the person in question.' For the first time, he thought of his birth mother in a way that wasn't exclusively abstract, wasn't merely a jigsaw piece that had to be located and slotted in for the completed picture.

What did she look like? Tall, short, fat, thin…? And from whom had he inherited his non-Irish looks? His adoptive parents had both been small, neat and fair-haired. He had towered above them, dark-haired, dark-eyed, olive-skinned...as physically different from them as chalk from cheese.

He stamped down his surge of curiosity and reminded himself that he wasn't here to form any kind of relationship with the woman but merely finally to lay an uncertain past to rest. Anger, curiosity and confusion were unhappy life companions and the faster he dispensed with them, the better.

'You're very suspicious, Leo.' Brianna thought back to his vehement declaration that women couldn't be trusted when it came to contraception. 'Everyone loves Bridget.'

'You mentioned that she didn't have a...partner.' A passing remark on which Brianna had not elaborated. Now, Leo was determined to prise as much information out of her as he could, information that would be a useful backdrop for when he met the woman the following day. It was a given, he recognised, that some people might think him heartless to extract information from the woman he was sleeping with, but he decided to view that as a necessity—something that couldn't be helped, something to be completely disassociated from the fact that they were lovers, and extremely passionate lovers at that.

Life, generally speaking, was all about people using people. If he hadn't learned that directly from his adoptive parents, then he certainly must have had it cemented somewhere deep within his consciousness. Perhaps, and in spite of his remarkably stable background, the fact that he was adopted had allowed a seed of cynicism to run rampant over the years.

'She doesn't talk much about that.'

'No? Why not? You're her…what would you say…confidante? I would have thought that she would find it a comfort to talk to you about whatever happened. I mean, you've known each other how long? Were your parents friends with the woman?'

Brianna laughed. 'Oh, gosh, no!' She glanced round the kitchen, making sure that all her jobs were done. 'Bridget is a relative newcomer to this area.'

'Really…' Leo murmured. 'I was under the impression that she was a valued, long-standing member of the community.' He almost laughed at the thought of that. Valued member of the community? Whilst jettisoning an unwanted child like an item of disposable garbage? Only in a community of jailbirds would someone like that have been up for consideration as a valued member.

'But now you tell me that she's a newcomer. How long has she been living in the area?'

'Eight years tops.'

'And before that?'

Brianna shot him a look of mild curiosity but, when he smiled that smile at her, that crooked, sexy half-smile, she felt any niggling questions hovering on the tip of her tongue disappear.

'You're asking a lot of questions,' she murmured breathlessly. He signalled for her to come closer and she did, until he could wrap his arms around her and hold her close.

'Like I said, I have a curious mind.' He breathed in the clean floral scent of her hair and for a few seconds forgot everything. 'You shouldn't have put your jumper back on,' he remarked in a voice that thrilled her to the core. 'I like looking at your breasts. Just the perfect mouthful…'

'And I have calls to make if I'm to keep the pub shut!' She slapped away his wandering hand, even though she would have liked nothing more than to drag him up to the bedroom to lay claim to him. 'And you have a book to work on!'

'I'd rather work on you…'

'Thank goodness Bridget isn't here. She'd be horrified.'

Leo nearly burst out laughing. 'And is this because she's the soul of prurience? You still haven't told me where she came from. Maybe she was a nun in her former life?' He began strolling out of the kitchen towards the sitting room with the open fire which he had requisitioned as his working space. His computer was shut and there was a stack of novels by the side of it, books he had picked from her collection. He had already started two, abandoned them both and was reaching the conclusion that soul-searching novels with complicated themes were not for him.

'There's no need to be sarcastic.' Brianna hovered by the table as he sat down. She knew that he demanded complete privacy when he was writing, sectioning off a corner of the sitting area, his back to the window. Yet somehow it felt as though their conversation was not quite at an end, even though he wasn't asking any further questions.

'Was I?'

His cool, dark eyes rested on her and she flushed and traced an invisible pattern with her finger on the table. Was there something she was missing? Some important link she was failing to connect?

'You've known this woman for a few years…'

'Nearly seven. She came to the pub one evening on her own.'

'In other words, she has a drinking habit?'

'No! She'd moved to the area and she thought it might be a way of meeting people! We have quiz nights here once a month. She used to come for the quiz nights, and after a while we got chatting.'

'Chatting about where she had come from? Oh

no; of course, you know nothing about that. And
I'm guessing not many clues as to what she was
doing here either? It's a small place for a woman
who wants to meet people...'

'It's a community. We make outsiders feel welcome.' She blushed at her unwitting choice of
words. 'I felt sorry for her,' Brianna continued
hurriedly. 'I started an over-forties' quiz night,
ladies only, so that she could get talking to some
of them.'

Leo was mentally joining the dots and was arriving at a picture not dissimilar to the one he had
always had of the woman who had given birth
to him—with a few extra trimmings thrown in
for good measure.

A new life and a new start for someone with a
dubious past to conceal. Tellingly, no one knew
about this past life, including the girl who had
supposedly become her anchor in the community.

It didn't take a genius to figure out that, where
there were secrets that required concealment,
those secrets were dirty little ones. He had re-
ceived half a picture from Brianna, he was certain of it—the rosy half, the half that didn't
conform to his expectations.

'And you did all this without having a clue as
to this woman's past?'

'I don't need to know every single detail about
someone's past to recognise a good person when

I see one!' She folded her arms tightly around her and glared down at him. She should have let him carry on with his writing. Instead, she had somehow found herself embroiled in an argument she hadn't courted and was dismayed at how sick it made her feel. 'I don't want to argue with you about this, Leo.'

'You're young. You're generous and trusting. You're about to give house room to someone whose past is a mystery.' He drew an uneasy parallel with his own circumstance, here at the pub under a very dubious cloud of deceit indeed, and dismissed any similarities. He was, after all, as upstanding and law-abiding as they came. No shady past here.

On the very point of tipping over into anger that he was in the process of dismissing her as the sort of gullible fool who might be taken in by someone who was up to no good, another thought lodged in the back of her mind. It took up residence next to the pernicious feel-good seed that had been planted when she had considered the possibility that he might not be welcoming Bridget because he cherished their one-to-one solitude.

Was he seriously *worried* about her? And if he was… That thought joined the other links in the chain that seemed to represent the nebulous beginnings of a commitment…

She knew that she was treading on very dangerous ground even having these crazy day dreams but she couldn't push them away. With her heart beating like a jack hammer, she attempted to squash the thrilling notion that he was concerned about her welfare.

'Do you think that my friend might be a homicidal maniac in the guise of a friendly and rather lonely woman?'

Leo frowned darkly. Brianna's thoughts about Bridget were frankly none of his concern, and irrelevant to the matter in hand, but he couldn't contain a surge of sudden, disorienting protectiveness.

Brianna had had to put her dreams and ambitions on hold to take charge of her father's failing business, whilst at the same time trying to deal with the double heartbreak of her father's death and her lover's abandonment. It should have been enough to turn her into an embittered shrew. Yet there was a transparent openness and natural honesty about her that had surfaced through the challenging debris of her past. She laughed a lot, she seldom complained and she was the sort of girl who would never spare an act of kindness.

'When people remove themselves for no apparent reason to start a new beginning, it's usually because they're running away from something.'

'You mean the police?'

Leo shrugged and tugged her towards him so that she collapsed on his lap with a stifled laugh. 'What if she turns into an unwanted pub guest who overstays her welcome?' He angled her so that she was straddling him on his lap and delicately pushed up the jumper.

'Don't be silly,' Brianna contradicted him breathlessly. 'You should get down to your writing. I should continue with my stock taking…'

In response to that, Leo eased the jumper off and gazed at her small, pert breasts with rampant satisfaction. He began licking one of her nipples, a lazy, light, teasing with the tip of his tongue, a connoisseur sampling an exquisite and irresistible offering.

'She has a perfectly nice little house of her own.' There was something wonderfully decadent about doing this, sitting on his lap in the middle of the empty pub, watching him as he nuzzled her breast as if he had all the time in the world and was in no hurry to take things to the next level.

'But—' Leo broke off. 'Here…' he flicked his tongue against her other nipple '…she would have…' he suckled for a few seconds, drawing her breast into his mouth '…you…' a few kisses on the soft roundness until he could feel her shiver and shudder '…to take care of her; cook her food…'

He held one of her breasts in his hand so that it was pushed up to him, the nipple engorged and throbbing, and he delicately sucked it. 'Brianna, she might seem perfectly harmless to you.' With a sigh, he leaned back in the chair and gave her tingling breasts a momentary reprieve. 'But what do you do if she decides that a cosy room in a pub, surrounded by people and hands-on waitress service, is more appealing than an empty house and the exertion of having to cook her own food?'

At no point was he inclined to give the woman the benefit of the doubt. In his experience, people rarely deserved that luxury, and certainly not someone with her particular shady history.

Never one ever to have been possessive or protective about the women in his life, he was a little shaken by the fierce streak suddenly racing through him that was repelled by the thought of someone taking advantage of the girl sitting on his lap with the easy smile, the flushed face and tousled hair.

'You need to exercise caution,' he muttered grimly. He raked his fingers through his hair and scowled, as though she had decided to disagree with him even though she hadn't uttered a word.

'Then maybe,' Brianna teased him lightly, 'you should stick around and make sure I don't end up becoming a patsy...'

The journey here should have taken no time at

all; his stay should have been over in a matter of a couple of days. There were meetings waiting for him and urgent trips abroad that could only be deferred for so long. It had never been his intention to turn this simple fact-finding exercise into a drama in three parts.

'Maybe I should,' he heard himself say softly. 'For a while…'

'And you can chase her away if she turns out to be an unscrupulous squatter who wants to take advantage of me.' She laughed as though nothing could be more ridiculous and raised her hand to caress his cheek.

Leo circled her slim wrist with his fingers in a vice- like grip. 'Oh, if she tries that,' he said in a voice that made her shiver, 'she'll discover just what a ruthless opponent I could prove to be—and just how regrettable it can be to cross my path.'

CHAPTER FIVE

THE SNOW HAD stopped. As grey and leaden as
the skies had been for a seemingly unstoppable
length of time, the sun now emerged, turning a
bleak winter landscape into a scene from a movie:
bright-blue skies and fields of purest white.

Bridget's arrival had been delayed by a day,
during which time Leo had allowed the subject
of her dubious, unknown past to be dropped. No
more hassle warning Brianna about accepting
the cuckoo in the nest. No more words of caution that the person she might have considered
a friend and surrogate mother might very well
turn out to be someone all set to take full advantage of her generous nature and hospitality. There
would be fallout from this gesture of putting the
woman up while she recuperated; he was certain
of that and he would be the man to deal with it.
So he might never have specialised in the role of
'knight in shining armour' in his life before, but
he was happy with his decision.

London would have to take a little back seat

for a while. He was managing to keep on top of things just fine via his computer, tablet and smartphone and, if anything dramatic arose, then he could always shoot down to sort it out.

All told, the prospect of being holed up in the middle of nowhere was not nearly as tedious as he might have imagined. In fact, all things considered, he was in tremendously high spirits.

Of course, Brianna was a hell of a long way responsible for that. He glanced up lazily from his computer to the sofa where she was sitting amidst piles of paperwork. Her hair was a rich tumble over her shoulders and she was cross-legged, leaning forward and chewing her lip as she stared at her way-past-its-sell-by-date computer which was on the low coffee table in front of her.

In a couple of hours the ambulance would be bringing his destiny towards him. For the moment, he intended to enjoy his woman. He closed the report in front of him and stood up, stretching, flexing his muscles.

From across the small, cosy room, Brianna looked up and, as always happened, her eyes lingered, absorbing the beautiful sight of his long, lean body; the way his jeans rode low on his hips; the way he filled out her father's checked flannel shirt in just the right way. He had loosely rolled the sleeves to his elbow and his strong, brown forearms, liberally sprinkled with dark hair, sent a little shiver of pleasurable awareness rippling through her.

'You should get a new computer.' Leo strolled towards her and then stood so that he was looking down at the columns of numbers flickering on the screen at him. 'Something faster, more up-to-date.'

'And I should have a holiday, somewhere warm and far away… And I'll do both just as soon as I have the money.' Brianna sighed and sat back, keenly aware of him looking over her. 'I just want to get all this stuff out of the way before Bridget gets here. I want to be able to devote some quality time to her.'

Leo massaged her neck from behind. Her hair, newly washed, was soft and silky. The baggy, faded pink jumper was the most unrevealing garment she could have worn but he had fast discovered that there was no need for her to wear anything that outlined her figure. His imagination was well supplied with all the necessary tools for providing graphic images of her body that kept him in a state of semi-permanent arousal.

'Was the urgent trip to the local supermarket part of the quality-service package?' He moved round to sit next to her, shoving some of the papers out of the way and wondering how on earth she could keep track of her paperwork when there seemed to be no discernible order to any of it.

'I know you don't agree with what I'm doing; I know you think I should just leave her to get on with things on her own but—'

'This conversational road is guaranteed to lead to a dead end,' he drawled smoothly. 'Let's do ourselves a favour and not travel down it.'

'You enjoyed the supermarket experience.' Brianna changed the subject immediately. She didn't want an argument. She didn't even want a mild disagreement, and she knew what his feelings were on the subject of their soon-to-be visitor, even though he had backed off from making any further disparaging remarks about her naïvety in taking in someone whose entire life hadn't been laid out on a plate for her perusal.

'It was…novel.' Actually, Leo couldn't recall the last time he had set foot in a supermarket. He paid someone to deal with the hassle of all that.

'Margaret Connelly has only just opened up that place. Actually, it's not a supermarket as such.'

'I'd noticed.'

'More of a…a…'

'Cosy space filled to overflowing with all manner of things, of which food is only one component? Brussels sprouts nestling next to fishing tackle…?'

'The lay out can seem a bit eccentric but the food's all fresh and locally sourced.'

Leo grinned, swivelled her so that she had her back to him and began massaging her shoulders. 'You sound like an advertisement for a food magazine. I'm going to have to put my foot down if you're thinking of slaving over a hot stove preparing dishes on this woman's whim.'

Brianna relaxed into the massage and smiled with contentment. She felt a thrill of pleasure at the possessive edge to his voice. 'She has to be on a bland diet—doctor's orders.'

'That's irrelevant. You're not going to be running up and down those stairs because someone rings a bell and wants a cup of tea immediately.'

'*You* could always do the running for me if you think I'm too fragile to cope.'

Leo's lips curled with derision and he fought down the impulse to burst into sardonic laughter. 'Running and doing errands for people isn't something I do.'

'Especially not in this instance,' Brianna said, remembering that he *was*, after all, a paying guest despite their unusual arrangement. He had given her a shocking amount of money for his stay thus far, way too much, and had informed her that it was something to do with company expenses owed to him before he'd quit his job. She hadn't quite understood his explanation. Nor had he backed down when she refused to take the full amount.

'Take it,' he had ordered, 'Or I'll just have to find another establishment that will accommodate what I want to pay. And I shall end up having to take taxis here to see you. You wouldn't want to add that further cost to a poor, struggling writer, would you?'

'What do you mean?' Leo stilled now.

'I mean you're a customer. Running up and down stairs isn't something I would ask you to do. That would be ridiculous. I would never take advantage of you like that.'

'But you *would* take advantage of me in other ways…because I happen to enjoy you taking advantage of me in all those other imaginative ways of yours…'

'Is *sex* all you ever think about?' she murmured, settling back against him and sighing as he slipped his hands underneath her jumper to fondle her breasts.

No. Sex most certainly had never been *all* he thought about. In fact, Leo contemplated with some bemusement, although he had always enjoyed an exceptionally varied and active sex life it had never been at the top of his priorities. Sex, and likewise women, had always taken a back seat to the more important driving force in his life, which was his work.

'You bring out the primitive in me,' he said
softly into her ear. 'Is it my fault that your body
drives me insane?' He relaxed into the sprawling
sofa so that he had Brianna half-lying on top of
him, her back pressed against his torso, her hair
tangled against his chest. He removed one hand
to brush some of her hair from his cheek and
returned his hand to her jeans to rest it lightly
on her hip. A stray sheet of paper wafted to the
ground, joining a disconcerting bundle already
there.

Brianna's body was responding as it always
did, with galloping excitement and sweet anticipation. She might very well joke that sex was the
only thing on his mind, but it certainly seemed to
have taken over all her responses as well. Even
the problem supplier she knew she had to deal
with urgently was forgotten as she undid the button and zip of her jeans.

'Tut, tut, tut; you're going to have to do better
than that, my darling. How am I expected to get
my hand where it wants to be?'

Brianna giggled softly. He had no hang-ups
about where they made love. His lack of inhibi-
tion was liberating and it worked in tandem with
her own period of celibacy to release an explosion
of passion she had never experienced in her life
before. She couldn't seem to get enough of him.

She wriggled out of her jeans and he chuckled.

'For someone with a body like yours, I'm always amazed that you've stuck to the functional underwear...' He thought about seeing her in something small, lacy and sexy, lying in his super-king-sized bed in his penthouse apartment in Chelsea.

The thought was random, springing from nowhere and establishing itself with such graphic clarity that he drew in his breath sharply with shock.

Hell, where was his mind going? This was a situation that was intensely enjoyable but it only functioned within very definite parameters. Like it or not, they were operating within a box, a box of his own making, and freedom from that box in any way, shape or form was a possibility that was not to be entertained.

With that in mind, he cleared his head of any inappropriate, wandering thoughts about her being in his apartment. Crazy.

'Is that how you like your women?' Brianna asked casually. He never spoke about his love life. A sudden thought occurred to her and, although this hardly seemed the time for a deep, meaningful conversation, she had to carry on regardless. 'Is that why you're here?'

'What are you talking about?'

Brianna wriggled so that she was on her side, still nestled between his legs, and she looked up at him, breathing in that clean, tangy scent that always seemed to scramble all her thoughts. His hand was curved on her hip, fingers dipping against her stomach. Even that small, casual contact did devastating things to her already hot, aroused body. She was slippery and wet, and it was mad, because she had to get things together before Bridget arrived.

'You know, all the way from London.'

'No clue as to what you're talking about.'

'Never mind. We need to start tidying up.' She sighed. 'Bridget's going to be here soon.'

'Didn't they say that they would telephone you before they left the hospital?'

'Yes, but…'

'No phone call yet.' After the disturbing tangent his thoughts had taken only moments before when he had imagined her in his apartment, the last thing Leo wanted was a heart-to-heart. He wanted to touch her; touching her was like a magic antidote to thinking. Hell, he had worked while he had been here, but his mind had not been on the cut and thrust of business deals with its customary focus. This was as close to a holiday as he had had in years, and the last thing he had expected when he had started on this journey of discovery.

He reached under her knickers, a dull beige with not a scrap of lace in sight, and slid his finger against the wet crease, seeking out the little nub of her clitoris. This was so much better than talking and a damn sight more worthwhile than the sudden chaos of thoughts that had earlier afflicted him.

Brianna moaned softly as he continued to rub. She squirmed and sighed and half-closed her eyes, her nostrils flaring and her breathing thickening the closer she came to a point of no return.

Questions still hovered at the back of her mind like pesky insects nipping at her conscience, refusing to go away, but right now she couldn't focus on any of that. Right now, as the movement of his strong, sure hand picked up speed, she moaned and arched her body and wave upon wave of pleasure surged through her. Lying with her back to him, she couldn't see his face, only his one hand moving inside her while the other was flattened against her thigh and his legs, spread to accommodate her body between them. But she knew that he was watching her body as he brought her to orgasm and the thought of that was wantonly exciting.

She was aware of her uneven, shaky breathing as she lay back and let her heated body return to planet Earth.

For a few seconds, there was silence. Leo linked his fingers on her stomach and absently noted the way they glistened with her honeyed wetness.

'I'm going to start clearing all my paperwork away,' she said eventually. 'I don't seem to have made much progress with our snack supplier. I'm going to have a shower.' She eased herself over his legs and off the sofa, and began tidying the papers which were strewn everywhere. She didn't bother to put on her jeans, instead choosing to scoop them up and drape them over one arm.

It all came down to sex. She knew that she was being silly for objecting to that because this was a situation that was never going to last longer than two minutes. It was something she had jumped into, eyes wide open, throwing caution to the winds and accepting it for what it was, and there was no excuse now for wanting more than what had been laid on the table.

Except…had she thought that this perfect stranger would possess the sort of complex personality that she would end up finding strangely compulsive?

Could she ever have imagined that an unexpected, astounding, elemental physical attraction would turn into something that seemed to have her in its hold? That taking a walk on the wild side, breaking out of the box for just a little while, would have repercussions that struck a chord of fear into her?

She wanted more. She couldn't even begin to think of him leaving, carrying on with his travels. He had entered her life, and what had previously been bland, dull and grey was now Technicolor-bright. She alternated between reading all sorts of things behind his words and actions and then telling herself that she really shouldn't.

'You never said…' Brianna begin heading up the stairs, carrying as much with her as she could: files, her jeans and her trainers, which she didn't bother to stick on completely.

Behind her, Leo scooped up the remainder of the files and began following her.

'Never said what?'

'All those women you're so cynical about…' She paused to look at him over her shoulder. 'The ones who wear lacy underwear…'

'Did I ever say that? I don't recall.'

'You didn't have to. I can read between the lines.' She spun back round and headed towards her suite of rooms, straight to the study, where she dumped all the files she had been carrying. She stood back and watched as he deposited the remainder of them, including her computer, which was as heavy as a barrow full of bricks, and—yes, he was right—in desperate need of updating.

Brianna took in his guarded, shuttered expression and knew instinctively that she was tread-

ing on quicksand, even though he hadn't rushed
in with any angry words telling her to mind her
own business. She could see it on his face. Her
heart was beating so fiercely that she could almost hear it in the still quiet of the room.

'I'm going to have a shower,' she mumbled,
backing out of the little office. 'On my own, if
you don't mind.'

Leo frowned and raked his fingers through his
hair, but he didn't move a muscle.

She wanted to *talk*. Talk about what? His exes?
What was the point of that? When it came to
women and meaningful conversations, they in-
variably led down the same road: a dead end. He
wasn't entirely sure where his aversion to commitment came from and he knew, if he were honest, that his parents would have wanted to see
him travel down the traditional route of marriage
and kids by thirty—but there it was; he hadn't.
He had never felt the inclination. Perhaps a feeling of security was something that developed in
a mother's womb and having been given up for
adoption, by definition, had wiped that out and
the security of making money, something tangible he could control, had taken its place.

At any rate, the minute any woman started
showing signs of crossing the barriers he had
firmly erected around himself, they were rele-
gated to history.

He told himself that there should be no difficulty in this particular relationship following the same course because he could see, from the look in her eyes, that whatever chat she wanted to have was not going to begin and end with the choice of underwear his women were accustomed to wearing.

He told himself that in fact it would be *easier* to end this relationship because, in essence, it had never really functioned in his real life. It had functioned as something sweet and satisfying within a bubble. And within a day or two, once he had met his birth mother and put any unanswered questions to rest, he would be gone.

So there definitely was *no* point to a lengthy heart-to-,heart. He strolled into the bedroom and glanced down at the snow which was already beginning to thaw.

She emerged minutes later from the shower with a towel wrapped round her, her long hair piled up on top of her head and held in place with a hair grip. Tendrils had escaped and framed her heart-shaped face. She looked impossibly young and vulnerable.

'What are you doing in my bedroom?'

'Okay. So I go out with women who seem to spend a lot of money on fancy underwear.' He glowered at her. 'I don't know what that has to do with anything.' He watched as she rummaged in her drawers in silence and fetched out some faded jogging bottoms and a rugby-style jumper, likewise faded.

Brianna knew that a few passing remarks had escalated into something that she found unsettling. She didn't want to pry into his life. She wanted to be the adult who took this on board, no questions asked and no strings attached. Unfortunately…

She disappeared back into the bathroom, changed and returned to find him still standing in an attitude of challenging defensiveness by the bedroom window.

'You wanted to talk…' he prompted, in defiance of common sense. 'Are you jealous that I've had lovers? That they've been the sort of women who—?'

'Don't run pubs, live on a shoestring and wear functional underwear from department stores? No, I'm not jealous. Why would I be?'

'Good. Because, personally, I don't do jealousy.' It occurred to Leo that there were a number of things he didn't do when it came to his personal relationships and yet, here he was, doing one of them right now: having a *talk*.

'Have we ended up in bed because you think I make a change?' She took a deep breath and looked him squarely in the face. He was so beautiful. He literally took her breath away. 'From all those women you went out with?' If *she* found him beautiful, if he blew *her* mind away, then why wouldn't he have had the same effect on hordes of other women?

'No! That's an absurd question.'

'Is it?' She turned on her heel and began back down the stairs to the bar area where she proceeded to do some unnecessary tidying. He lounged against the bar, hands in his pockets, and watched her as she worked. She appeared to be in no hurry to proceed with the conversation she had initiated. The longer the silence stretched between them, the more disgruntled Leo became.

Moving to stand directly in front of her, so that she was forced to stop arranging the beer mats in straight lines on the counter, he said, 'If there's any comparison to be done, then you win hands down.'

Brianna felt a stupid surge of pleasure. 'I'm guessing you *would* say that, considering we're sleeping together and you're pretty much stuck here.'

'Am I? The snow seems to be on its way out.' They weren't touching each other, but he could feel her as forcibly as if they had been lying naked on her bed.

'How long do you intend to stay?' She flushed and glanced down at her feet before taking a deep breath and looking at him without flinching. 'I'm going to keep the pub closed for another fortnight but just in case, er, bookings come in for the rooms, it would be helpful for me to know when yours might be free to, er, rent out…'

And this, Leo thought, was the perfect opportunity to put a date in the calendar. It was as obvious as the nose on his face that her reason for wanting to find out when he would be leaving had nothing to do with a possible mystery surge in bookings for the rooms. He didn't like being put in a position of feeling trapped.

'I told you I'd stick around, make sure you didn't get ripped off or taken advantage of by this so-called best buddy of yours,' he said roughly. 'I won't be going anywhere until I'm satisfied that you're okay on that score. Satisfied? No; you're not. What else is on your mind, Brianna? Spit it out and then I can disappear for a shower and some work and leave you to get on with your female bonding in peace.'

Brianna shrugged. Everything about his body language suggested that he was in no mood to stand here, answering questions. Perhaps, she thought, answering questions was something else he *didn't do* when it came to women. Like jealousy. And yet he wasn't moving. 'Did you end up here on the back of a bad relationship?' she asked bluntly. She shot him a defiant look from under her lashes. 'I know you don't want me to ask lots of questions…'

'Did I ever say that?'

'You don't have to.'

'Because, let me guess, you seem to have a hot line to my thoughts!' He scowled. Far from backing away from an interrogation he didn't want and certainly didn't need, his feet appeared to be disobeying the express orders of his brain. Against all odds, he wanted to wipe that defensive, guarded expression from her face. 'And no, I did not end up here on the back of a bad relationship.' He had ended up here because…

Leo flushed darkly, uncomfortable with where his thoughts were drifting.

'I'm sleeping with you, and I know it's going to end soon, but I still want to know that you're not using me as some sort of sticking plaster while you try to recover from a broken heart.'

'I've never suffered from a broken heart, Brianna.' Leo smiled crookedly at her and stroked the side of her face with his finger.

Just then her mobile buzzed and after only a few seconds on the phone she said to him, 'Bridget's had her final check-up with the consultant and they're going to be setting off in about half an hour. They'll probably be here in about an hour and a half or so. Depends on the roads, but the main roads will all be gritted. It's only the country lanes around here that are still a little snowed up.'

An hour and a half. Leo's lips thinned but, despite the impending meeting with his mother, one which he had quietly anticipated for a number of years ever since he had tracked down her whereabouts, his focus remained exclusively on the girl standing in front of him.

'Everyone has suffered from a broken heart at some point.' She reverted to her original topic.

'I'm the exception to the rule.'

'You've never been in love?'

'You say that as though it's inconceivable. No. Never. And stop looking at me as though I've suddenly turned into an alien life-form. Are you telling me that, after your experience with the guy you thought you would be spending your life with, you're still glad to have *been in love*?'

He lounged against the bar and stared down at her. He had become so accustomed to wearing jeans and an assortment of her father's old plaid flannel shirts, a vast array of which she seemed to have kept, that he idly wondered what it would feel like returning to his snappy handmade suits, his Italian shoes, the silk ties, driving one of his three cars or having Harry chauffeur him. He would return to the reality of high- powered meetings, life in the fast lane, private planes and first-class travel to all four corners of the globe.

Here, he could be a million miles away, living on another planet. Was that why he now found himself inclined to have this type of conversation? The sort of touchy-feely conversation that he had always made a point of steering well clear from? Really, since when had he ever been into probing any woman about her thoughts and feelings about past loves?

'Of course I am,' Brianna exclaimed stoutly. 'It may have crashed and burned, but there were moments of real happiness.'

Leo frowned. Real happiness? What did she mean by that? Good sex? He didn't care much for a trip down happiness lane with her. If she felt inclined to reminisce over the good old days, conveniently forgetting the misery that had been dished up to her in the end, then he was not the man with the listening ear.

'How salutary that you can ignore the fact that you were taken for a ride for years… Are you still in touch with the creep?'

Brianna frowned and tried to remember what the creep looked like. 'No,' she said honestly. 'I haven't got a clue what he's up to. The last I heard from one of my friends from uni, he had gone abroad to work for some important law firm in New York. He's disappeared completely. I was heartbroken at the time, but it doesn't mean that I'm not glad I met him, and it doesn't mean that I don't hope to meet that someone special at some point in the future.'

And as she said that a very clear picture of Mr Special floated into her mind. He was approximately six-two with bronzed skin, nearly black hair and lazy, midnight-dark eyes that could send shivers racing up and down her spine. He came in a package that had carried very clear health warnings but still she had fallen for him like a stupid teenager with more hormones than common sense.

Fallen *in lust* with him, she thought with feverish panic. She hadn't had a relationship with a guy for years! And then he had come along, drop-dead gorgeous, with all the seductive anonymity of a stranger—a writer, no less. Was it any wonder that she had fallen *in lust* with him?

Was that why she could now feel herself becoming *clingy*? Not wanting him to go? Losing all sense of perspective?

'And no one special is on the scene here?' Leo drawled lazily. 'Surely the lads must be queuing up for you…'

Of course there had been nibbles, but Brianna had never been interested. She had reasoned to herself that she just didn't have the time; that her big, broken love affair had irreparably damaged something inside her; that, just as soon as the pub really began paying its way, she would jump back into the dating world.

All lies. She could have had all the time in the world, a fully paid-up functioning heart and a pub that turned over a million pounds a year in profit and she still wouldn't have been drawn to anyone—because she had been waiting for just the moment when Leo Spencer walked through the door, tall, dark and dangerous, like a gunslinger in a Western movie.

'I'm not interested in anything serious at the moment,' she said faintly. 'I have loads of time. Bridget should be arriving any minute now.'

'At least an hour left to go…' How was it possible to shove all thoughts of his so-called mother out of his head? He had almost forgotten that the woman was on her way.

'I need to go and get her room ready.'

'Haven't you already done that? The potpourri and the new throw from the jack-of-all-trades supermarket?'

She had. But suddenly she wanted nothing more than to escape his suffocating masculine presence, find a spot where she could straighten out her tangled thoughts.

'Well, I want to make sure that it's just right,' she said sharply.

Leo stepped aside. 'And I think I'll go and have

a shower and do something productive with my time in my room.'

'You don't have to disappear! You're a paying guest, Leo. You can come down and do your writing in your usual place. Bridget and I won't make any noise at all. She'll probably just want to rest.'

'I'll let the two of you do your bonding in peace,' he murmured. 'I'll come down for dinner. I take it you'll be cooking for three?'

'You know I will, and please don't start on the business of me being a mug.'

Leo held up both hands in a gesture of mock-indignation that she could even contemplate such a thing.

Brianna shot him a reluctant smile. 'You wait and see. You'll end up loving her as much as I do.'

'Yes. We'll certainly wait and see,' Leo delivered with a coolness that Brianna felt rather than saw, because his expression was mildly amused. She wondered if she had perhaps imagined it.

Leo remained where he was while she disappeared upstairs to do her last check of the bedroom where Bridget would be staying, doubtless making sure that the sheets were in place with hospital precision, corners tucked in just so.

His mouth curled with derision. The thought of her being taken advantage of filled him with disgust. The thought of her putting her trust in a woman who would inevitably turn out not to be the person she thought she was made his stomach turn. He could think of no other woman whose trusting nature should be allowed to remain intact.

He slammed his clenched fist against the wall and gritted his teeth. He had come here predisposed to dislike the woman who had given birth to him and then given him away. He was even more predisposed to dislike her as the woman who, in the final analysis, would reveal her true colours to the girl who had had the kindness to take her under her wing.

The force of his feelings on this subject surprised him. It was like the powerful impact of a depth charge, rumbling down deep in the very core of him.

He didn't wait for the ambulance bearing his destiny towards him to arrive, instead pushing himself away from the wall and heading up to his bedroom. His focus on work had been alarmingly casual and now, having had a shower, he buried himself in reports, numbers, figures and all the things that usually had the ability to fully engage his attention.

Not now. His brain refused to obey the commands being issued to it. What would the woman look like? Years ago, he could have had pictures taken of her when he had set his man on her trail, but he hadn't bothered because she had been just a missing slot in his life he had wanted to fill. He hadn't given a damn what she looked like. Now, he had to fight the temptation to stroll over to the window and peer out to the courtyard which his room overlooked.

He stiffened when he eventually heard the sound of the ambulance pulling up and the muffled rise and fall of voices which carried up to his room.

Deliberately he tuned out and exerted every ounce of will power to rein in his exasperating, wandering mind.

At a little after five, he got a text from Brianna: a light early supper would be served at six. If he wanted to join them, then he was more than welcome. Sorry she couldn't come up to his room but she had barely had time to draw breath since Bridget had arrived.

She had concluded her text with a smiley face. Who *did* that? He smiled and texted back: yes, he'd be down promptly at six.

He sat back and stared at the wall. In an hour he would meet his past. He would put that to bed and then, when that was done, he would move on, back to the life from which he had taken this brief respite.

He had an image of Brianna's face gazing at

him, of her lithe, slim body, of the way she had
of humming under her breath when she was oc-
cupied doing something, and the way she looked
when she was curled up on the sofa trying to
make sense of her accounts.

But of course, he thought grimly, that was fine.
Sure, she would be on his mind. They might not
have spent a long time in each other's company
but it had been concentrated time. Plenty long
enough for images of her to get stuck in his head.

But she was not part of his reality. He would
check out the woman who had given birth to him,
put his curiosity to bed and, yes, move on…

CHAPTER SIX

LEO WASN'T QUITE sure when the snow had stopped, when the furious blizzards had turned to tamer snowfall, and when that tamer snowfall had given way to a fine, steady drizzle that wiped clean the white horizon and returned it to its original, snow-free state.

He couldn't quite believe that he was still here. Of course, he returned to London sporadically mid-week and was uncomfortably aware of his conscience every time he vaguely intimated that there were things to do with the job he had ditched: paperwork that needed sorting out; problems with his accommodation that needed seeing to; social engagements that had to be fulfilled because he should have returned to London by now.

The lie he had blithely concocted before his game plan had been derailed did not sit quite so easily now. But what the hell was he to do?

He rose to move towards the window and stared distractedly down at the open fields that backed the pub. It was nearly three. In three hours, the pub would be alive with the usual Friday evening crowd, most of whom he knew by sight if not by name.

How had something so straightforward become so tangled in grey areas?

Of course, he knew. In fact, he could track the path as clearly as if it was signposted. His simple plan—go in, confirm all the suspicions he had harboured about his birth mother, close the book and leave—had slipped out of place the second he had been confronted with Brianna.

She was everything the women he had dated in the past were not. Was that why he had not been able to kill his ill-advised temptation to take her to bed? And had her natural, open personality, once sampled, become an addiction he found impossible to jettison? He couldn't seem to see her without wanting her. She turned him on in ways that were unimaginable. For once in his life, he experienced a complete loss of self-control when they made love; it was a drug too powerful to resist.

And then…his mother. The woman he had prejudged, had seen as no more than a distasteful curiosity that had to be boxed and filed away, had not slotted neatly into the box he had prepared.

With a sigh, he raked his fingers through his hair and glanced over his shoulder to the reports blinking at him, demanding urgent attention, yet failing to focus it.

He thought back to when he had met her, that very first impression: smaller than he'd imagined, clearly younger, although her face was worn, very frail after hospital. He had expected someone brash, someone who fitted the image of a woman willing to give away a baby. He had realised, after only an hour in her company, that his preconceived notions were simplistic. That was an eventuality he had not taken into account. He lived his life with clean lines, no room for all those grey areas that could turn stark reality into a sludgy mess. But he had heard her gentle voice and, hard as he had tried not to be swayed, he had found himself hovering on the brink of needing to know more before he made his final judgement.

Not that anything she had said had been of any importance. The three of them had sat on that first evening and had dinner while Brianna had fussed and clucked and his mother had smiled with warm sympathy and complained about her garden and the winter vegetables which would sadly be suffering from negligence.

She had asked him about himself. He had looked at her and wondered where his dark eyes and colouring came from. She was slight and blonde with green eyes. At one point, she had murmured with a faraway expression that he reminded her of someone, someone she used to know, but he had killed that tangent and moved the conversation along.

Seeing her, meeting her, had made him feel weird, confused, uncomfortable in his own skin. A thousand questions had reared their ugly heads and he had killed them all by grimly holding on to his anger. But underneath that anger he had known only too well that the foundations on which he had relied were beginning to feel shaky. He had no longer known what he should be feeling.

Since that first day, he had seen her, though, only in brief interludes and always with Brianna around. Much of the time she spent in her bedroom. She was an avid reader. He had had to reacquaint himself with literature in an attempt to keep his so-called writer occupation as credible as possible. He had caught himself wondering what books she enjoyed reading.

On his last trip to London, he had brought with him a stack of books and had been surprised to discover that, after a diet of work-related reading, the fiction and non-fiction he had begun delving into had not been the hard work he had expected. And at least he could make a halfway decent job of sounding articulate on matters non-financial.

Where this was going to lead, he had no idea.

He headed downstairs and pulled up short at the sight of Bridget sitting in the small lounge set aside from the bar area, which Brianna had turned into her private place if she didn't want to remain in her bedroom.

Because of Bridget, the pub now had slightly restricted opening and closing hours. He assumed that that was something that could only be achieved in a small town where all the regulars knew what was going on and would not be motivated to take their trade elsewhere—something that would have been quite tedious, as 'elsewhere' was not exactly conveniently located to get to by foot or on a bike.

'Leo!'

Leo paused, suddenly indecisive at being confronted by his mother without Brianna around as an intermediary. She was sitting by the large bay window that overlooked the back garden and the fields behind the pub. Her fair hair was tied back and the thin, gaunt lines of her face were accentuated so that she resembled a wraith.

'Brianna's still out.' She patted the chair facing hers and motioned to him to join her. 'We haven't chatted very much at all. Why don't you have a cup of tea with me?'

Leo frowned, exasperated at his inability to take control of the situation. Did he want to talk to his mother on a one-to-one basis? Why did he suddenly feel so...*vulnerable* and at odds with himself at the prospect? Wasn't this why he had descended on this back-of-nowhere town in the first place? So things had not turned out quite as he had anticipated, but wasn't it still on his agenda to find out what the woman was like?

He was struck by the unexpectedly fierce urge to find out what had possessed her to throw him to the wolves.

He thought that perhaps the facade she portrayed now was a far cry from the real person lurking underneath, and he hardened himself against the weak temptation to be swept along into thinking that she was innocent, pathetic and deserving of sympathy. Could it be that, without Brianna there to impress, her true colours would be revealed?

'I think I'll have black coffee myself. Would you like to switch to coffee?'

'No, my dear, my pot of tea will be fine, although perhaps you could refresh the hot water. I feel exhausted if I'm on my feet for too long and I've been far too active today for my own good.'

He was back with a mug of coffee and the newly refreshed pot of tea which he rested on the table by her, next to the plate of biscuits which were untouched.

'I'm so glad I've caught you on your own,' she murmured as soon as he had taken a seat next to her. 'I feel I barely know you and yet Brianna is so taken with you after such a short space of time.'

'When you say "taken with me"...' He had told Brianna that he saw it as his duty to keep an eye on her houseguest, to scope her out, because a houseguest with a mysteriously absent past was not a houseguest to be trusted. Was the houseguest doing the same with him? He almost laughed out loud at the thought. As always when he was in her company, he had to try not to stare, not to try and find similarities...

'She's, well, I suppose you know about...'

'About the guy who broke her heart when she was at university?'

'She's locked herself away for years, has expressed no interest in any kind of love life at all. I've always thought it sad for someone so young and caring and beautiful, that she wouldn't be able to share those qualities with a soul mate.'

Leo said something and nothing. He looked at the cane leaning against the chair and wondered what it must feel like to be relatively young and yet require the assistance of a walking stick.

'If you don't mind my asking, how old are you, Bridget?'

Bridget looked at him in surprise. 'Why do you ask?'

Leo shrugged and sipped his coffee.

'Not yet fifty,' Bridget said quietly. 'Although I know I look much, much older.' She glanced away to stare through the window and he could see the shine of unshed tears filming her eyes.

In his head, he was doing the maths.

'But we weren't talking about me,' she said softly.

Leo felt a surge of healthy cynicism and thought that if she figured she could disappear behind a veil of anonymity then she was in for a surprise. There were things he wanted to find out, things he *needed* to find out, and he knew himself well—what he wanted, he got, be it money, women or, in this case, answers. The unsettling hesitancy that had afflicted him off and on, the hesitancy he hated because he just wasn't a hesitant person, thankfully disappeared beneath the weight of this new resolve.

'Indulge me,' he said smoothly. 'I hate one-sided conversations. I especially hate long chats about myself… I'm a man, after all. Self-expression is a luxury I don't tend to indulge very often. So, let's talk about you for a minute. I'm curious. You're not yet fifty, you tell me? Seems very young to have abandoned the lure of city lights for a quiet place like this.' He still could not quite believe that she was as young as she said. She looked like a woman in her sixties.

'What you may call "quiet", by which I take it you mean "dull", is what I see as peace.'

'Brianna said that you've been here a while— quite a few years; you must have been even younger when you decided that you wanted "peace".' He couldn't help thinking that, although their colouring was different, he had her eyes, the shape of them. He looked away with a frown.

She blushed and for the first time he could see her relative youth peep out from behind the care-worn features.

'My life's been…complicated. Not quite the life I ever expected, matter of fact.'

Curiosity was gnawing at him but he kept his features perfectly schooled, the disinterested by-stander in whom he hoped she would confide. He could feel in his bones that the questions he wanted answering were about to be answered.

'Why don't you talk about it?' he murmured, resting the cup on the table and leaning towards her, his forearms resting on his thighs. 'You probably feel constrained talking to Brianna. In such a small, close-knit community perhaps you didn't want your private life to be thrown into the public arena?' He could see her hesitate. Secrets were always burdensome. 'Not that Brianna would ever be one to reveal a confidence, but one can never be too sure, I suppose.'

'And who knows how long I have left?' Bridget

said quietly. She plucked distractedly at the loose gown she was wearing and stared off through the window as though it might offer up some inspiration. 'My health isn't good: stress, built up over the years. The doctor says I could have another heart attack at any time. They can't promise that the next time round won't be fatal.' She looked at him pensively. 'And I suppose I wouldn't want to burden Brianna with my life story. She's a sweet girl but I would never want to put her in a position of having to express a sympathy she couldn't feel.'

Or pass judgement which would certainly mean the end of your happy times with her, Leo thought with another spurt of that healthy cynicism, cynicism he knew he had to work at.

'But I don't come from here…' he encouraged in a low voice.

'I grew up in a place not dissimilar to this,' she murmured. 'Well, bigger, but not by a lot. Everybody knew everybody else. All the girls knew the boys they would end up marrying. I was destined for Jimmy O'Connor; lived two doors away. His parents were my parents' best friends. In fact, we were practically born on the same day, but that all went up the spout when I met Robbie Cabrera. *Roberto* Cabrera.'

Leo stilled. 'He was Spanish?'

'Yes. His father had come over for a temporary job on a building site ten miles out of town. Six months. He was put into our school and all the girls went mad for him. I used to be pretty once, when I was a young girl of fifteen…you might not guess it now.' She sighed and looked at him with a girlish smile which, like that blush, brought her buried youth back up to the surface.

'And what happened?' Leo was surprised he could talk so naturally, as though he was listening to someone else's story rather than his own.

'We fell madly in love. In the way that you do when you're young and innocent.' She shot him a concerned looked and he hastened to assure her that whatever she told him would stay with him. Adrenaline was pumping through him. He hadn't experienced this edge-of-the-precipice feeling in a very long time. If ever. This was why he was here. The only reason he was here.

From nowhere, he had a vision of Brianna laughing and telling him that there was nothing more satisfying than growing your own tomatoes in summer, and teasing him that he probably wouldn't understand because he probably lived in one of those horrible apartment blocks where you wouldn't be able to grow a tomato if your life depended on it.

He thought of himself, picking her up then and hauling her off to his bedroom at a ridiculous hour after the pub had finally been closed.

Thought of her curving, feline smile as she lay on his bed, half-naked, her small, perfect breasts turning him on until his erection felt painful and he couldn't get his clothes off fast enough.

'Sorry?' He leaned in closer. 'You were saying…?'

'I know. You're shocked. And I don't mean to shock you but it's a relief to talk about this; I haven't with anyone. I fell pregnant. At fifteen. My family were distraught, and of course there was no question of abortion, not that we would have got rid of it. No, Robbie and I were committed to one another.'

'Pregnant…'

'I was still a child myself. We both were. We wanted to keep it but my parents wouldn't allow it. I was shipped off to a convent to give birth.'

'You wanted to keep it?'

'I never even held it. Never knew if it was a boy or a girl. I returned to Ireland, went back to school, but from that moment on my parents were lost to me. I had three younger siblings and they never knew what had happened. Still don't. Family life was never the same again.'

'And the father of the child?'

Bridget smiled. 'We ran away. His father ended up on a two-year contract. We skipped town when we were sixteen and headed south. I kept my parents informed of my whereabouts but I couldn't see them and they never lived down the shame of what I'd done. I don't think they cared one way or the other. Robbie always kept in touch with his parents and in fact, when they moved to London, we stayed with them for several months before they returned to Spain.'

'You…ran away…' For some reason, his normally agile mind seemed to be lagging behind.

'We were very happy, Robbie and me, for over twenty years until he died in a hit-and-run accident and then I went back to Ireland. Not back to where I grew up, but to another little town, and then eventually I came here.'

'Hit and run…' The tidal rush of emotions was so intense that he stood up and paced like a wounded bear, before dropping back into the chair.

'We never had any more children. Out of respect for the one I was forced to give up for adoption.'

Suddenly the room felt too small. He felt himself break out in a fine perspiration. Restless energy poured through him, driving him back onto his feet. His cool, logical mind willed him to stay put and utter one or two platitudes to bring the conversation to a satisfactory conclusion. But the chaotic jumble of thoughts filling every corner of his brain was forcing him to pace the room, his movements uncoordinated and strangely jerky.

He was aware of Bridget saying something, murmuring, her face now turned to the window, lost in her thoughts.

There was so much to process that he wasn't sure where to start. So this was the story he had been waiting for and the ending had not been anticipated. She hadn't been the convenient stereotype he had envisaged: she wasn't the irresponsible no-hoper who had given him away without a backward glance. And, now that he knew that, what the hell happened next?

He turned to her, saw that she had nodded off and almost immediately heard the sound of Brianna returning.

'What's wrong?' About to shut the door, Brianna stood still and looked at him with a concerned frown. She had been out shopping and had had to force herself to take her time, not to hurry back, because she just wanted to *see* him, to *be* with him. 'Is…is Bridget all right?' She walked towards him and he automatically reached out to help her with the bags of shopping. Brianna stifled the warm thrill that little slice of pretend domesticity gave her.

'Bridget is fine. She appears to have fallen asleep. Have you ever…?' Leo murmured, reaching to cup the nape of her neck so that he could pull her towards him. 'Thought that you were going in one direction, only to find that the signposts had been switched somewhere along the way and the destination you were heading to turned out to be as substantial as a mirage?'

Brianna's heart skipped a beat. Was he talking about *her*? she wondered with heightened excitement. Was he trying to tell her that meeting her had derailed him? She placed her hand flat on his chest and then slipped it between two buttons to feel his roughened hair.

'What are you saying?' she whispered, wriggling her fingers and undoing the buttons so that she could now see the hard chest against which her fingers were splayed.

'I'm saying I want to have sex with you.' And right at that moment it really was exactly what he wanted. He wanted to drown the clamour of discordant voices in his head and just make love to her. With the bags of shopping in just one hand, he nudged her towards the kitchen.

'We can't!' But her hands were scrabbling over him, hurrying to undo the buttons of his shirt, and her breasts were aching in anticipation of being touched by him. 'Bridget…'

'Asleep.' He shut down the associated thoughts that came with mention of her name.

'I've got to start getting ready to open up.'

'But not for another half-hour. I assure you…' They were in the kitchen now and he kicked the door shut behind him and pushed her towards the wall until she was backed up against it. 'A lot can be accomplished in half an hour.'

The low drawl of intent sent delicious shivers racing up and down her spine and she groaned as he unzipped her jeans and pushed his hand underneath her panties. Frustrated because his big hand couldn't do what it wanted to do thanks to the tightness of her jeans, he yanked them down, and Brianna quickly stepped out of them.

Bridget, she thought wildly, would have another heart attack if she decided to pop into the kitchen for something. But fortunately her energy levels were still very low and if she was asleep then she would remain asleep at least for another hour or so.

Her fingers dug into his shoulders and she uttered a low, wrenching groan as he pulled the crotch of her panties to one side and began rubbing her throbbing clitoris with his finger.

Her panties were damp with her arousal. She gave a broken sigh and her eyelids fluttered. She could feel him clumsily undoing his trousers and then his thick hardness pushing against her jumper.

This was fast and furious sex.

Where was his cool? Leo was catapulted right back to his days of being a horny teenager lacking in finesse, except he couldn't remember, even as a horny teenager, being as wildly out of control as he was now. He didn't even bother with taking off her jumper, far less his. He hooked his finger under her knickers and she completed the job of disposing of them. He could barely get it together to don protection. His hand was shaking and he swore in frustration as he ripped open the packet.

Then he took her. He hoisted her onto him and thrust into her with a grunt of pleasurable release. Hands under her buttocks, he pushed hard and heard her little cry of pleasure with intense satisfaction.

They came together, their bodies utterly united, both of them oblivious to their surroundings.

He dropped her to the ground, his breathing heavy and uncontrolled. 'Not usually my style.' But, as he watched her wriggle back into her underwear and jeans, he figured it could well become part of his repertoire without a great deal of trouble.

'You look a little hot and flustered.' He gently smoothed some tendrils of hair away from her face and Brianna added that tender gesture to the stockpile she was mentally constructing. She felt another zing of excitement when she thought back to what he had said about his plans not going quite as he had anticipated. She would have loved nothing more than to quiz him further on the subject, but she would let it rest for the moment. One thing she had learnt about him was that he was not a man who could be prodded into saying anything or doing anything unless he wanted to.

'Right—the bar. I need to get going. I need to check on Bridget.'

Plus a million and one other things that needed doing, including sticking away the stuff she had bought. All that was running through her head as a byline to the pleasurable thought of the big guy behind her admitting to wanting more than a passing fling. A nomad would one day find a place to stay put, wouldn't he? That was how it worked. And, if he didn't want to stay put *here*, then she would be prepared to follow him. She knew she would.

Her mind was a thousand miles away, so it took her a few minutes to realise that something was wrong when she entered the little lounge to check on Bridget.

She should have been in the chair by the window. It was where she always sat, looking out or reading her book. But she wasn't there. Her mind moved sluggishly as she quickly scanned the room and she saw the limp body huddled behind the chair about the same time as Leo did.

It felt like hours but in fact it could only have been a matter of seconds, and Leo was on it before her brain had really had time to crank into gear. She was aware of him gently inspecting Bridget while barking orders to her at the same time: make sure the pub was shut; fetch some water; get a blanket; bring him the telephone because his mobile phone was in his bedroom, then amending that for her to fetch his mobile phone after all.

'I'll call an ambulance!'

'Leave that to me.'

Such was his unspoken strength that it didn't occur to her to do anything but as he said. She shut the pub. Then it was upstairs to fetch his mobile phone, along with one of the spare guest blankets which she kept in the airing cupboard, only stopping en route to grab a glass of water from the kitchen.

'She's breathing,' was the first thing he said when she returned. 'So don't look so panicked.' He gestured to his phone, scrolled down and began dialling a number. She couldn't quite catch what he was saying because he had walked over to the window and was talking in a low, urgent voice, his back to her. Not that she was paying any attention. She was loosely holding Bridget, talking to her in soft murmurs while trying to assess what the damage was. It looked as though she had fallen, banged her head against the table and passed out. But, in her condition, what could be the ramifications of that?

'Right.' Leo turned to her and slipped the

mobile phone into his jeans pocket. 'It's taken care of.'

'Sorry?'

'It's under control. The main thing is to keep her still. We don't know what she's broken with that fall.'

'I'm glad you said that it was a fall. That's what I thought. Surely that must be less serious than another heart attack. Is the ambulance on its way? I've made sure the "closed" sign's on the front door. When I get a chance, I'll ring round a couple of the regulars and explain the situation.'

Leo hesitated. 'No ambulance.'

Brianna looked at him, startled. 'But she's got to go to hospital!'

'Trust me when I tell you that I have things under control.' He squatted alongside them both. The time of reckoning had come and how on earth had he ever played with the thought that it wouldn't? How had he imagined that he would be able to walk away without a backward glance when the time came?

Of course, he certainly hadn't reckoned on the time coming in this fashion. He certainly hadn't thought that he would be the one rescuing his mother because it now seemed that there was more conversation left between them.

'You have things under control?' Brianna

looked at him dubiously. 'And yet there's no ambulance on the way?'

'I've arranged to have her air-lifted to the Cromwell Hospital in London,' Leo said bluntly.

'I beg your pardon?'

'It should be here any minute soon. In terms of timing, it will probably get here faster than an ambulance would, even an ambulance with its sirens going.'

In the midst of trying to process what sounded like complete gibberish to her, Brianna heard the distant sound of an overhead aircraft. Landing would be no problem. In fact, there couldn't have been a better spot for an air ambulance to land. The noise grew louder and louder until it felt as though it would take the roof off the pub, and then there was a flurry of activity while she stood back, confused.

She became a mystified bystander as the professionals took over, their movements hurried and urgent, ferrying Bridget to the aircraft.

Then Leo turned to her. 'You should come.'

Brianna looked at him in complete silence. 'Leo…what's going on?' How had he managed to do *that*? Who on earth could arrange for someone to be airlifted to a hospital hundreds of, miles away? She had thought that maybe he had been in computers, but had he been in the medical field? Surely not. She was uneasily aware that there were great, big gaps in her knowledge about him but there was little time to think as she nodded and was hurried along to the waiting aircraft.

'I don't have any clothes.'

'It's not a problem.'

'What do you mean, it's *not a problem*?'

'We haven't got time to debate this. Let's go.'

Brianna's head was full of so many questions, yet something in her resisted asking any of them. Instead she said weakly, as they were lifted noisily into the air and the aircraft swung sharply away, leaving the pub behind, 'Do you think she'll be all right?' And then, with a tremulous laugh, because the detachment on his dark face filled her with a dreadful apprehension, 'I guess this would make a fantastic scene in your book…'

Leo looked at her. She was huddled against him and her open, trusting face was shadowed with anxiety.

This was a relationship that was never going to last. They had both been aware of that from the very start. He had made the position perfectly clear. So, in terms of conscience, he was surely justified in thinking that his was completely clear? But it still took a great deal of effort to grit his teeth and not succumb to a wave of unedited, pure regret for what he knew now lay on the horizon. But this wasn't the time to talk about any of this so he chose to ignore her

quip about the book that was as fictitious as the
Easter Bunny.

'I think she'll be fine but why take chances?'

'Leo…'

'We'll be at the hospital very shortly, Brianna.'
He sighed deeply, pressed his thumbs against his
eyes and then rested his head against the upright,
uncomfortable seat. 'We'll talk once Bridget's
settled in hospital.'

Brianna shivered as he looked away to stare
out of the window but she remained silent; then
there wasn't much time to do any thinking at all
as everything seemed to happen at once and with
impressive speed.

Once again she stood helplessly on the sidelines and watched as the machinery of the medical world took over. She had never seen anything
like it and she was even more impressed at Leo's
handling of the situation, the way he just seemed
to take charge, the way he knew exactly what to
do and the way people appeared to listen to him
in a way she instinctively knew they wouldn't
have to anyone else.

Like a spare part, she followed him into the
hospital, which was more like a hotel than anything else, a hotel filled with doctors and nurses,
somewhere designed to inspire confidence. The
smallness of her life crowded her as she watched,
nervously torn between wanting to get nearer to

Bridget, who had now been established in a room of her own, and wanting to stay out of the way just in case she got mown down by the crisp efficiency of everyone bustling around their new patient.

It felt like ages until Bridget was examined, wheeled off for tests and examined again. Leo was in the thick of it. She, on the other hand, kept her distance and at one point was firmly ushered to a plush waiting room, gently encouraged to sit, handed a cappuccino and informed that she would help matters enormously if she just relaxed, that everything was going to be perfectly fine.

How on earth was she supposed to relax? she wondered. Not only was she worried sick, but alongside all her concerns about her friend other, more unsettling ideas were jostling in her head like pernicious, stinging insects trying to get a hold.

She was dead on her feet by the time Leo finally made an appearance and he, too, looked haggard. Brianna half-rose and he waved her back down, pulled one the chairs across and sat opposite her, legs apart, his arms resting loosely on his thighs.

More than anything else, she wanted to reach out and smooth away the tired lines around his eyes and she sat on her hands to avoid giving in to the temptation which here, and now, seemed horribly inappropriate.

'Leo, what's going on?'

'The main thing is that Bridget is going to be okay. It seems she stood up and fell as she was reaching for her cane. She banged her head against the edge of the table and knocked herself out. They've done tests to make sure that she suffered no brain damage and to ascertain that the shock didn't affect her heart.' He looked at her upturned face and flushed darkly.

'I'm amazed you rushed into action like that when she could have just gone to the local hospital.' She reached out tentatively to touch his arm and he vaulted upright and prowled through the shiny, expensive waiting room of which they were the only occupants.

'Brianna...' He paused to stare down at her and all of a sudden there was no justification whatsoever for any of the lies he had told. It didn't matter whether they had been told in good faith, whether the consequences had been unforeseen. Nor did the rights and wrongs of sleeping with the girl, now staring up at him, come into play.

'It's late. You need to get some rest. But more importantly we have to talk...'

'Yes.' Why was she so reluctant to hear what he had to say? Where was that gut reaction coming from?

'I'm going to take you back to my place.'

'I beg your pardon? You still have a place in London? What place? I thought you might have sold that—you know?—to do your travelling.'

Leo shook his head and raked his fingers through his dishevelled hair. 'I think when we get there,' he said on a heavy sigh, 'some of the questions you're asking yourself might begin to fall into place.

CHAPTER SEVEN

BRIANNA'S FIRST SHOCK was when they emerged from the hospital and Leo immediately made a call on his mobile which resulted, five minutes later, in the appearance of a top-of-the range black Range Rover. It paused and he opened the back door for her and stood aside to allow her to slide into the luxurious leather seat.

Suddenly she was seeing him in a whole new light. He was still wearing the jeans in which he had travelled, a long-sleeved jumper and one of the old coats which he had found in a cupboard at the back of the pub and which he had adopted because it was well lined. But even with this casual clothing he now seemed a different person. He was no longer the outdoor guy with that slow, sexy smile that dragged on her senses. There was a harshness to his face that she was picking up for the first time and it sent a shiver of apprehension racing up and down her spine.

The silence stretched on and on as the car

slowly pulled away from the kerb and began heading into central London.

When she looked over to him, it was to quail inwardly at the sight of the forbidding cast of his features, so she pretended to be absorbed in the monotonous, crowded London landscape of pavements and buildings.

It was very late but, whereas in Ireland the night sky would be dense and black at this hour and the countryside barely visible, here the street-lights illuminated everything. And there were people around: little groups shivering on the pavements, the odd business man in a suit and, the further towards the centre of London the car went, the busier the streets were.

Where one earth were they going? So he had a house in London. Why had he never mentioned that? Her mind scrabbled frantically to come up with some logical reason why he might have kept it a secret. Perhaps he was in the process of selling it. Everyone knew that it could take for ever to sell a property and, if he *was* selling it, then maybe he thought that there was no point mentioning it at all. But when she glanced surreptitiously at his forbidding profile, all the excuses she tried to formulate in her head withered and died.

'Where are we going? I know you said your house, but where exactly is that?'

Leo shifted and angled his body so that he was facing her. Hell, this was a total mess; he could only lay one-hundred per cent of the blame for that at his own door. He had behaved like a stupid fool and now he was about to be stuck handling the fallout.

Brianna was a simple country girl. He had known that the second he had seen her. She might have had the grit and courage to single-handedly run a pub, but emotionally she was a baby, despite her heartbreak. She was just the sort of woman he should have steered clear from, yet had he? No. He had found that curious blend of street-wise savvy and trusting naivety irresistible. He had wanted her and so he had taken her. Of course, she had jumped in to the relationship eyes wide open, yet he couldn't help but feel that the blame still lay entirely on his shoulders. He had been arrogant and selfish and those qualities, neither of which had caused him a moment's concern in the past, now disgusted him.

He harked back to his conversation with Bridget. Before it had turned to the illuminating matter of her past, she had wanted to talk to him about Brianna, had opened the subject by letting on that Brianna hadn't been involved with anyone since her loser boyfriend from university had dumped her. Leo now followed the path of that conversation which had never got off the starting blocks as it turned out.

Had she been on the brink of confiding just how deeply Brianna was involved with him?

Of course she had been! Why kid himself? He might have laid down his ground rules and told her that he was not in the market for involvement, but then he had proceeded to demonstrate quite the opposite in a hundred and one ways. He couldn't quite figure out how this had happened, but it had, and the time had come to set the matter straight.

'Knightsbridge,' he told her, already disliking himself for the explanation he would be forced to give. Less than twenty-four hours ago they had been making love, fast, furious love, her legs wrapped around him, as primitive and driven as two wild animals in heat. The memory of it threatened to sideswipe him and, totally inexplicably, he felt himself harden, felt his erection push painfully against his zip so that he had to shift a little to alleviate the ache.

'Knightsbridge. Knightsbridge as in *Harrods*, Knightsbridge?' The last time Brianna had been to London had been three years ago, and before that when she had been going out with Daniel. She would have had to be living on another planet not to know that Knightsbridge was one of the most expensive parts of London, if not the most expensive.

'That's right.' On cue, the gleaming glass building in which his duplex apartment was located rose upwards, arrogantly demanding notice, not that anyone could fail to pay attention and salute its magnificence.

He nodded towards it, a slight inclination of his head, and Brianna, following his eyes, gasped in shock.

'My apartment's there,' he told her and he watched as the colour drained away from her face and her eyes widened to huge, green saucers.

Before she could think of anything to say, the chauffeur-driven Range Rover was pulling smoothly up in front of the building and she was being ushered out of the car, as limp as a rag doll.

She barely noticed the whoosh of the lift as it carried them upwards. Nor did she take in any of her surroundings until she was finally standing in his apartment, a massive, sprawling testimony to the very best money could buy.

With her back pressed to the door, she watched as he switched on lights with a remote control and dropped blinds with another remote before turning to her with his thumbs hooked into the pockets of his jeans.

They stared at each other in silence and he finally said, the first to turn away, 'So this is where

I live. There are five bedrooms. It's late; you can hit the sack now in one of them, or we can talk'

'You actually *own* this place?' Her gaze roamed from the slate flooring in the expansive hall to the white walls, the dark wood that replaced the slate and the edge of a massive canvas she could glimpse in what she assumed would be another grand space—maybe his living room.

'I own it.' He strolled through into the living area, which had been signposted by that glimpse of wall art. Following behind him, Brianna saw that it was a massive piece of abstract art and that there were several others on the walls. They provided the only glimpse of colour against a palette that was uniformly white: white walls, white rug against the dark wooden floor, white leather furniture.

'I thought you were broke.' Brianna dubiously eyed the chair to which she was being directed. She yawned and he instantly told her that she should get some rest.

'I'd prefer to find out what's going on.'

'In which case, you might need a drink.' He strolled towards a cabinet and she looked around her, only to refocus as he thrust a glass with some amber liquid into her hand.

He sat down next to her and leaned forward, cradling his drink while he took in her flushed face. He noticed that she couldn't meet his eyes and he had to steel himself against a wave of sickening emotion.

'We should never have slept together,' he delivered abruptly and Brianna's eyes shot to his.

'What do you mean?'

'I mean…' He swirled his drink round and then swallowed a long mouthful. Never had he needed a swig of alcohol more. 'When I arrived in Ballybay, it was not my intention to get involved with anyone. It was something that just seemed to happen, but it could have and should have been prevented. I blame myself entirely for that, Brianna.'

Hurt lanced through Brianna. Was this the same guy about whom she had been nurturing silly, girlish daydreams involving an improbable future? One where he stuck his hat on the door and decided to stay put, so that they could explore what they had? She felt her colour rise as mortification kicked in with a vengeance.

'And why is that?'

'Because I knew you for what you were, despite what you said. You told me that you were tough, that you weren't looking for anything committed, that you wanted nothing more from me than sex, pure and simple. I chose to believe you because I was attracted to you. I chose to ignore the voice of reason telling me that you weren't half as tough as you claimed to be.' Even now—and he could see her stiffening as she absorbed what he was saying—there was still a softness to her mouth that belied anything hard.

He found that he just couldn't remain sitting next to her. He couldn't feel the warmth she was radiating without all his thoughts going into a tailspin.

'I'm pretty tough, Leo. I've been on my own for a long time and I've managed fine.'

Leo prowled through the room, barely taking in the exquisite, breathtakingly expensive minimalist décor, and not paying a scrap of attention to the Serpentine glittering hundreds of metres in the distance, a black, broad stripe beyond the bank of trees.

'You've taken over your father's pub,' he said heavily, finishing the rest of his drink in one long gulp and dumping the glass on the low, squat table between the sofa and the chairs. It was of beaten metal and had cost the earth. 'You know how to handle hard work, but that's not what I'm talking about and we both know that. I told you from the start that I was just passing through and that hasn't changed. Not for me. I'm…I'm sorry.'

'I understood the rules, Leo.' Her cheeks were stinging and her hands didn't want to keep still. She had to grip the glass tightly to stop them from shaking. 'I just don't get…' she waved her hand to encompass the room in which they were sitting, with its floor-to-ceiling glass windows, its expensive abstract art and weirdly soulless, uncomfortable furniture '...all of this. What sort of job did you have before?'

Leo sighed and rubbed his eyes. It was late to begin this conversation. It didn't feel like the right time, but then what *would* be the right time? In the morning? The following afternoon? A not-so-distant point in the future? There *was* no right time.

'No past tense, Brianna.'

'Sorry?'

'There's no past tense. I never gave my job up.' He laughed mirthlessly at the notion of any such thing ever happening. He was defined by his work, always had been. Apart from the past few weeks, when he had played truant for the first time in his life.

'You never gave your job up...but...?'

'I run a very large and very complex network of companies, Brianna. I'm the boss. I own them. My employees report to me. That's why I can afford all of this, as well as a house in the Caribbean, an apartment in New York and another in Hong Kong. Have another sip of that drink. It'll steady your nerves. It's a lot to take in, and I'm sorry about that, but like I said I never anticipated getting in so deep...I never thought that I would have to sit here and have this conversation with you, or anyone else, for that matter.'

Brianna took a swig of the brandy he had poured for her and felt it burn her throat. She had a thousand angry questions running through her head but they were all silenced by the one, very big realisation—he had lied to her. She didn't know why, and she wasn't even sure that it mattered, because nothing could change the simple truth that he had lied. She felt numb just thinking about it.

'So you're not a writer.'

'Brianna, I'm sorry. No. The last time I did any kind of creative writing was when I was in school, and even then it had never been one of my stronger subjects.' She wasn't crying and somehow that made it all the harder. He had fired a lot of people in his time, had told aspiring employees that their aspirations were misplaced, but nothing had prepared him for what he was feeling now.

'Right.'

Unable to keep still, he sprang to his feet and began pacing the room. His thoughts veered irrationally, comparing the cold, elegant beauty of his sitting room and the warm, untidy cosiness of the tiny lounge at the back of her pub, and he was instantly angry with himself for allowing that small loss of self-control.

He had had numerous girlfriends in the past. He had always told them that commitment wasn't an option and, although quite a few had made the mistake of getting it into their heads that he might have been lying, he had never felt a moment's regret in telling the deluded ones goodbye.

'So what were you doing in Ballybay?' she asked. 'Did you just decide on the spur of the moment that you needed a break from…from the big apartment with the fancy paintings and all those companies you own? Did you think that you needed to get up close and personal with how the other half lives?'

She laughed bitterly. 'Poor Leo. What a blow to have ended up stuck in my pub with no mod cons, having to clear snow and help with the washing up. How you must have missed your flash car and designer clothes! I bet you didn't bank on having to stick around for as long as you did.'

'Sarcasm doesn't suit you.'

But he had flushed darkly and was finding it difficult to meet her fierce, accusatory green-eyed stare. 'I'm sorry,' Brianna apologised with saccharine insincerity. 'I find it really hard to be sweet and smiling when I've just discovered that the guy I've been sleeping with is a liar.'

'Which never made our passion any less incendiary.'

Her eyes tangled with his and she felt the hot, slow burn of an unwitting arousal that made her ball her hands into angry fists. Unbelievable: her body responding to some primitive vibe that was still running between them like a live current that couldn't be switched off.

'Why did you bother to make up some stupid story about being a writer?' she flung at him. 'Why didn't you say that you were just another rich businessman who wanted to spend a few days slumming it and winding down? Why the fairy story? Was that all part of the *let's adopt a different persona*?' She kept her eyes firmly focused on his face but she was still taking in the perfection of the whole, the amazing body, the strong arms, the length of his legs. Knowing exactly what he looked like underneath the clothes didn't help. 'Well?' she persisted in the face of his silence.

'The story is a little more complex than a bid to take time out from my life here...'

'What do you mean?' She was overwhelmed by a wave of giddiness. She couldn't tear her eyes away from his face and she found that she was sitting ramrod erect, as rigid as a plank of wood, her hands positioned squarely on her knees.

'There was a reason I came to Ballybay.' Always in control of all situations, Leo scowled at the unpleasant and uncustomary sensation of finding himself on the back foot. Suddenly the clinical, expensive sophistication of his surroundings irritated the hell out of him. It was an unsuitable environment in which to be having this sort of highly personal conversation. But would 'warm and cosy' have made any difference? He had to do what he had to do. That was just the way life was. She would be hurt, but she was young and she would get over it. It wasn't as though he had made her promises he had had no intention of keeping!

He unrealistically told himself that she might even *benefit* from the experience. She had not had a lover for years. He had crashed through that icy barrier and reintroduced her to normal, physical interaction between two people; had opened the door for her to move forward and get back out there in the real world, find herself a guy to settle down with…

That thought seemed spectacularly unappealing and he jettisoned it immediately. No point losing track of the moment and getting wrapped up in useless speculation and hypotheses.

'A reason?'

'I was looking for someone.' He sat heavily on the chair facing hers and, as her posture was tense and upright, so his was the exact opposite as he leaned towards her, legs wide apart, his strong forearms resting on his thighs. He could feel her hurt withdrawal from him and it did weird things to his state of mind.

'Who?'

'It might help if I told you a little bit about myself, Brianna.'

'You mean aside from the lies you've already told me?'

'The lies were necessary, or at least it seemed so at the time.'

'Lies are never necessary.'

'And that's a point we can possibly debate at a later date. For now, let me start by telling you that I was adopted at birth. It's nothing that is a state secret, but the reason I came to Ballybay is because I traced my birth mother a few years ago and I concluded that finding her was something I had to do. Not while my adoptive parents were still alive. I loved them very much; I would never have wanted to hurt them in any way.'

Brianna stared at him open-mouthed. It felt as though the connections in her brain were all backfiring so that nothing made sense any more. What on earth was he going on about? And how could he just *sit there* as though this was the most normal conversation in the world?

'You're adopted?' was all she could say weakly, because she just couldn't seem to join the dots in the conversation.

'I grew up in leafy, affluent suburbia, the only child of a couple who couldn't have children of their own. I knew from the beginning that I was adopted, and it has to be said that they gave me the sort of upbringing that most kids could only dream about.'

'But you didn't want to find your real mother until now?'

'*Real* mother is not a term I would use. And finding her would not have been appropriate had my adoptive parents still been alive. Like I said, I owe everything to them, and they would have been hurt had I announced that I was off on a journey of discovery.'

'But they're no longer alive. And so you decided to trace your…your…'

'I've had the information on the woman for years, Brianna. I simply bided my time.'

Brianna stared at him. He'd simply *bided his time*? There was something so deliberate and so controlled about that simple statement that her head reeled.

'And…and…you came to Ballybay and pretended to be someone you weren't because…?'

'Because it was smaller than I imagined,' he confessed truthfully. 'And I wanted to find out about the woman before I passed judgement.'

'You mean if you had announced yourself and told everyone why you were there…what? Your mother—sorry, your *birth* mother—would have tried to…to what?' She looked around her at the staggering, shameless testimony to his well-heeled life and then settled her eyes back on him.

'Did you think that you needed to keep your real identity a secret because if she knew how rich you were she would have tried to latch on to your money?'

Leo made an awkward, dismissive gesture with his hand. 'I don't allow people to latch on to my money,' he said flatly. 'No, I kept my identity a secret, as indeed my purpose in being there in the first place, because I wasn't sure what I would do with the information I gathered.'

'How can you talk about this with such a lack of emotion? I feel as though I'm seeing a stranger.'

Leo sat back and raked his fingers through his hair. He was being honest. In fact, he was sparing no detail when it came to telling the truth, yet he still felt like the guy wrecking Christmas by taking a gun to Santa Claus.

'A stranger you've made love to countless times,' he couldn't help but murmur in a driven undertone that belied his cool exterior. He took a deep breath and tried to fight the intrusive memory of his hands over her smooth, slender body, tracing the light sprinkling of freckles on her collarbone, the circular discs of her nipples and the soft, downy hair between her legs. She was the most naturally, openly responsive lover he had ever had. When he parted her legs to cup the moisture between them, he felt her responding one-hundred per cent to his touch. She didn't play games. She hadn't hidden how he had made her feel.

'And I wish I hadn't.' Brianna was momentarily distracted from the direction of their conversation.

'You don't mean that. Whatever you think of me now, your body was always on fire for mine!'

Again she felt that treacherous lick of desire speed along her nerve endings like an unwanted intruder bypassing all her fortifications. This was not a road she wanted to travel down, not at all. Not when everything was collapsing around her ears.

'And did you find her?' she asked tightly.

'I did,' he answered after only the briefest of hesitations.

'Who is she?'

'At the moment, she's lying in the Cromwell Hospital.'

Brianna half-stood and then fell back onto the chair as though the air had been knocked out of her lungs.

His mother was Bridget. Bridget McGuire. And all of a sudden everything began falling into place with sickening impact. Perhaps not immediately, but very quickly, he had ascertained that she knew Bridget, that she considered Bridget one of her closest friends. Try as she might, Brianna couldn't reference the time scale of this conversation. Had it happened *before* he'd decided to prolong his stay? Surely it would have?

That realisation was like a physical blow because with it came the inevitable conclusion that he had used her. He had wanted to find out about his mother and she had been an umbilical cord to information he felt he might have needed; to soften her up and raise no suspicions, he had assumed the spurious identity of a writer. When he had been sitting in front of his computer, she'd assumed that he had been working on his book. Now, as head of whatever vast empire he ran, she realised he would have been working, communicating with the outside world from the dreary isolation of a small town in Ireland he would never have deigned to visit had he not needed to.

How could she have been so stupid, so naive? She had swooned like a foolish sixteen-year-old the second she had clapped eyes on him and had had no qualms about justifying her decision to leap into bed with him.

She had been his satisfying bonus for being stuck in the boondocks.

'I didn't even know that Bridget had ever had children... Does she know?' Her voice was flat and devoid of any expression.

That, without the tears, told him all he needed to know about her state of mind. He had brought this on himself and he wasn't going to flinch from this difficult conversation. He told himself that there had never been any notion of a long-lasting relationship with her, yet the repetition of that mantra failed to do its job, failed to make him feel any better.

'No. She doesn't.'

'And when will you tell her?'

'When I feel the time is right.'

'If you wanted to find your mother and announce yourself—if you weren't suspicious that she would try and con money out of you—then why the secrecy? Why didn't you just do us all a favour: show up in your fancy car and present yourself as the long-lost prodigal son?'

'Because I didn't know what I was going to find, but I suspected that what I found would—how shall I put this?—not be to my liking.'

'Hence all your warnings about her when I told you that she was going to be coming to the pub to stay after her bout in hospital...' Brianna said slowly, feeling the thrust of yet another dagger deep down inside her. 'You knew she was hiding a past and you assumed she was a lowlife who would end up taking advantage of me, stealing from me, even. What changed?'

Leo shrugged and Brianna rose to her feet and managed to put distance between them. For a few seconds she stared down at the eerily lit landscape below her, devoid of people, just patches of light interspersed with darkness. Then she returned to the chair and this time she forced herself to try and relax, to give him no opportunity to see just how badly she was affected by what he had said to her.

'So you were using me all along,' she said matter-of-factly. 'You came to Ballybay with a purpose, found out that it wasn't going to be as straightforward as you anticipated—because it's the kind of small place where everybody knows everybody else, so you wouldn't be able to pass unnoticed, without comment—you adopted an identity and the second you found out that I knew your mother...sorry, your *birth mother*...you decided that it would be an idea to get to know me better.'

Leo's jaw hardened. Her inexorable conclusions left a bitter taste in his mouth but he wasn't going to rail against them. What was needed here was a clean break. If she had become too involved, then what was the point in encouraging further involvement by entering into a debate on what he had meant or not meant to do?

His failure to deny or confirm her statement was almost more than Brianna could bear but she kept her voice cool and level and willed herself just to try and detach from the situation. At least here, now; later, she would release the emotion that was building inside her, piling up like water constrained by paper-thin walls, ready to burst its banks and destroy everything in its path.

She could read nothing from his expression. Where was the guy she had laughed with? Made love to? Teased? Who was this implacable stranger sitting in front of her?

How, even more fatally, could she have made such a colossal mistake again? Misjudged someone so utterly that their withdrawal came as complete shock? Except this time it was all so much worse. She had known him for a fraction of the time she had known Daniel. Yet she knew, without a shadow of a doubt, that the impact Daniel had made on her all those years ago was nothing in comparison to what she would feel when she walked away from this. How was that possible? And yet she knew that what Leo had generated inside her had reached deeper and faster and was more profound in a million ways.

'I guess you decided that sleeping with me would be a good way to get background information on Bridget. Or maybe it was just something that was given to you on a silver platter.' Bitterness crept into her voice because she knew very well that what she said was the absolute truth. He hadn't had to energise himself into trying to get her into bed. She had leapt in before he had even finished asking the question.

'We enjoyed one another, Brianna. God, never have I apologised so much and so sincerely.'

'Except I wasn't using you.' She chose to ignore his apology because, in the big picture, it was just stupid and meaningless.

'I...' *Wasn't using you?* How much of that statement could he truthfully deny? 'That doesn't detract from the fact that what we had was real.'

'Don't you mean that the *sex* we had was real? Because beyond that we didn't have anything. You were supposed to be a writer travelling through, getting inspiration.' The conversation seemed to be going round and round in circles and she couldn't see a way of leading it towards anything that could resemble a conclusion. It felt like being in a labyrinth and she began walking on wooden legs towards her coat which she had earlier dumped on one of the chairs.

'Where are you going?'

'Where do you think, Leo? I'm leaving.'

'To go where? For God's sake, Brianna, there are guest rooms galore in this apartment. Pick whichever one you want to use! This is all a shock, I get that, but you can't just run out of here with nowhere to go!' Frustration laced his words with a savage urgency that made him darken and he sprang up, took a couple of steps towards her and then stopped.

They stood staring at one another. Her open

transparency, which was so much part and parcel of her personality, had been replaced by a frozen aloofness that was doing all sorts of crazy, unexpected things to his head. He was overcome with an uncontrollable desire to smash things. He turned sharply away. His head was telling him that if she wanted to go, then he should let her go, but his body was already missing the feel of hers and he was enraged with himself for being sidestepped by an emotion over which he appeared to have no control.

Brianna could sense the shift of his body away from her, even though she was trying hard not to actually look at him, and that was just a further strike of the hammer. He couldn't even look at her. She was now disposable, however much he had wanted her. He had found his mother, had had whatever conversation with her that had changed his mind about her, and now he had no further use for the woman he had taken and used.

'Well?' he demanded roughly. 'Where are you going to go at this hour? Brianna, please…'

She wanted to tell him that the last thing she could do was sleep in one of his guest bedrooms. Just the thought of him being under the same roof would have kept her up all night.

She backed towards the door. 'I'm going to go to the hospital.'

'And do *what* there, Brianna? Visiting hours

are well and truly over and I don't think they'll allow overnight guests in the common area.' He felt as though he was being ripped apart. 'You have my word that I won't come near you,' he said, attempting to soften his tone. 'I'll leave the apartment, if you want. Go stay in a hotel.'

Did he think that she was scared that he might try and break down her bedroom door so that he could ravish her? Did he honestly imagine that she was foolish enough to fear any such thing after what he had said?

'You can leave or you can stay, Leo.' She gave a jerky shake of her shoulder. 'I don't honestly care. I'm going to the hospital and, no, I won't be trying to cadge a night's sleep on the sofa in the common area. I'm going to leave a letter for one of the nurses to hand to Bridget in the morning, explaining that I've had to get back to the pub.'

'And the reason for that being…?' There were shadows under her eyes. He didn't feel proud to acknowledge the fact that he had put them there. His guilty conscience refused to be reined in. 'What reason could you have for needing to rush back to the pub? Or do you intend to tell Bridget the truth about who I am?'

'I would never do that, Leo, and the fact that you would think that I might just shows how little you know me. As little, as it turns out, I know you. We were just a couple of strangers having fun for a few weeks.' Her heart constricted painfully when she said that. 'I know you think that I'm all wrapped up in you, but I'm not. I'm upset because I didn't take you for a liar and, now that I know what you are, I'm glad this is all over. Next to you, Daniel was a walk in the park!'

For several reasons, none of which she intended to divulge, this was closer to the truth than he could ever imagine and she could see from his dark flush that she had hit home. He had been fond of referring to her distant ex as one of life's great losers.

She stuck her chin up and looked him squarely in the eyes without flinching. 'After I've been to the hospital, I shall find somewhere cheap to stay until I can catch the first train out of London.'

'This isn't Ballybay! London isn't safe at night to be wandering around in search of cheap hotels!'

'I'll take my chances!' Of course he would see no problem with her sleeping in his apartment, she thought with punishing reality. She meant nothing to him, so why on earth would he be affected by her presence? And, if that were the case, then wouldn't it be the same for her? 'And when I leave here I never, ever want to see you again.'

CHAPTER EIGHT

'DIDN'T THIS OCCUR to you at all, Miss Sullivan?'

Her doctor looked at her with the sort of expression that implied this was a conversation he had had many times before. Possibly, however, not with someone who was unmarried. Unmarried and pregnant in these parts was a rare occurrence.

Her head was swimming. It had been over a month since she had walked out of Leo's life for ever and in the interim she had heard not a word from him, although she had heard *about* him, thanks to Bridget, who emailed her regularly with updates on the joys of finding her long-lost son.

Bridget had remained in London in his apartment, where she had all the benefits of round-the-clock care and help courtesy of a man who had limitless funds. She hadn't even needed to fetch any of her clothes, as she was now the fortunate recipient of a brand-new wardrobe.

On all fronts, he was the golden child she thought she had lost for ever.

In between these golden tributes, Brianna never managed to get any answers to the questions she *really* wanted to ask, such as did he ever talk about her? Was he missing her? Was there someone else in his life?

And now *this*.

'No, not really.' Brianna found that she could barely enunciate the words. Pregnant. They had been so careful. Aside from that one time… She resisted the temptation to put her hand on her still flat stomach. 'I…I didn't even notice that I'd skipped a period…' Because she had been so wrapped up thinking about him, missing him, wishing he was still around. So busy functioning on autopilot that she had missed the really big, life-altering thing happening.

'And what will you do now, Brianna?

Brianna looked at the kindly old man who had delivered her and pretty much everyone her age in Ballybay and beyond.

'I'm going to have this baby, Dr Fallow, and I shall be a very proud, single mother.' She stuck her chin up defiantly and he smiled at her.

'I would have expected nothing less from Annie Sullivan's daughter. And the father?'

And the father…?

The question plagued her over the next few days. He deserved to know. Or did he? He had used her and then dispatched her once her usefulness was at an end. Did a man like that deserve to know that she was having his baby? He had been ultra-careful with precautions. How ironic that despite the best laid plans—because of a split condom, a one-in-a-million chance—here she was, the exception to the rule. And a cruel exception, because having a baby was not on his agenda, least of all with a woman he had used. So what would be his reaction should she show up on his doorstep with the happy news that he was going to be a daddy? She shuddered when she thought of it: horror, rage, shock. And, although there was no way he could blame her, he would still be upset and enraged that fate had dealt him a blow he couldn't deal with.

Yet, how could she *not* tell him? Especially given the circumstances of his adoption? Would he appreciate being left in the dark about his own flesh and blood? Perhaps finding out at some much later date down the road, and being destined forever to imagine that his son or daughter had grown up thinking of him as someone who had not taken enough interest to make contact? Being left in the awful position of wondering whether his own life story had been repeated, except without him even being aware of it?

The pros and cons ran through her head like a constant refrain, although beneath that refrain the one consolation was that she was in no doubt that she was happy about the pregnancy, however much it would disrupt her way of life. In fact, she was ecstatic. She had not thought about babies, having had no guy in her life with whom to have them. And, although she couldn't have chosen a less suitable candidate for the role of father, she was filled with a sense of joyous wonder at the life slowly growing inside her.

A life which would soon become apparent; pregnancy was not a condition that could be kept secret. Within a month or two, she would be the talk of the town, and of course Bridget would know. How could she fail to?

Which pretty much concluded her agonising. Leo would find out and she would have to be the one to tell him before he heard it second-hand.

It seemed the sort of conversation to be held in the evening and, before the bustle of the pub could begin, sweeping her off her feet, she got on the phone and dialled his mobile.

Around her, the pub lacked its usual shine and polish. She would have to start thinking about getting someone in to cover for her on a fairly permanent basis. There was no way she and Shannon could cope but there was also no way she could afford to close the pub, far less find a buyer for it.

Money, she foresaw, was going to be a head-ache and she gritted her teeth together because she knew what Leo's solution would be: fling money at the problem. Which would leave her continually indebted to him and that was not a situation that filled her with joy.

But then, she would never, ever be able to break contact with him from here on in, would she?

Even if he just paid the occasional visit in between running those companies of his, he would still be a permanent cloud on her horizon. She would have to look forward to seeing him moving on, finding other women, other women to whom he hadn't fabricated a convoluted story about himself. Eventually, she would have to witness his happiness as he found his soul mate, married her, had children with her. It didn't bear thinking about.

His disembodied voice, deep, dark and lazy, jolted her out of her daydreaming and fired up every nerve in her body. All at once, she could picture him in every vivid, unsettling detail: the way he used to look at her, half-brooding, full of sexy promise; the way he used to laugh whenever she teased him; the way the muscles of his amazing body rippled and flexed when he moved…

'It's me,' she said a little breathlessly, before clearing her throat and telling herself to get a grip.

'I know who it is, Brianna,' Leo drawled. He

rose to shut his office door. She had caught him
as he had been about to leave. Ever since his
mother had arrived on the scene and was recu-
perating happily at his apartment, he had been
leaving work earlier than normal. It was a change
of pattern he could not have foreseen in a million
years, but he was strangely energised by getting
to know his mother a little better. She could never
replace the couple who had adopted him, but she
was a person in her own right, and one he found
he wanted to get to know. It seemed that a ge-
netic link was far more powerful a bond than he
could ever have conceived possible.

He thought back to that moment when he had
sat next to her at her hospital bed and taken her
hand in his. An awkward moment and one he had
never envisaged but as she had lain there, frail
and bewildered at her expensive private room, it
had seemed right.

And he had told her—haltingly at first, trying
to find the words to span over thirty years. He
had watched her eyes fill up and had felt the way
her hand had trembled. He had never expected
his journey to take him there and he had been
shocked at how much it had changed his way of
thinking, had made him see the shades of grey
between the black and white. No one could ever
replace the wonderful parents he had had, but
a new road had opened up—not better, but dif-

ferent—and he had felt a soaring sense of fulfilment at what lay ahead. He had known that they both did.

For a man who had always known the way ahead, he had discovered the wonder of finding himself on a path with no signposts, just his feelings to guide him, and as he had opened up to his mother, asked her questions, replied to the hundreds she had asked him in return, he had turned a corner. The unknown had become something to be embraced.

'How's Bridget?'

'I thought you spoke and emailed daily?' He sat back down at his desk and swivelled his chair so that it was facing the broad floor-to-ceiling glass panes that overlooked the city.

'Why are you calling?' It had been more of a struggle putting her behind him than he could ever have believed possible. Was it because Bridget was staying with him? Because her presence kept alive memories he wanted to bury? He didn't know. Whilst his head did all the right things and told him that she no longer had a place in his life—that what they'd had had been good but it had never been destined to last—some irrational part of him insisted on singing a different tune.

He had found his concentration inexplicably flagging in the middle of meetings. On more than one occasion, he had awoken from a dream-filled sleep to find himself with an erection. Cold showers were becoming the rule rather than the exception. All told, he felt as though he was in unchartered territory. He was taking new steps with his mother and discovering that old ways of dealing with exes did not apply to Brianna.

He knew that she and Bridget were in touch by phone daily and it took every ounce of will-power not to indulge his rampant curiosity and try to prise information out of his house guest. What was she up to? Had she found a replacement for him in her bed? There was no denying that she was hot; what man wouldn't want to try his luck? And she was no longer cocooned within those glacial walls of celibacy. She had stepped out from behind them and released all the unbelievable passion he knew her to be capable of. There was no way that she could ever return to living life like a nun. And, however much she had or hadn't been wrapped up in him, she was ripe for a rebound relationship.

Was that what she was doing right now—engaging in wild sex with some loser from the town or another passing stranger?

He had never considered himself someone who was prone to flights of fancy, but he was making up for lost time now.

All of this introduced a level of coolness to his

voice as he stared out of the window and waited for her to come up with an answer.

She damn well wasn't phoning for an update on Bridget, so why was she?

Brianna picked up the unwelcoming indifference in his voice and it stung. Had he *completely* detached from her? How was that possible? And how was he going to greet what she had to tell him, were that the case?

'I...I...need to talk to you.'

'I'm listening. But make it quick. I was on my way out.'

'I need to see you...to discuss what I have to say.'

'Why?'

'Can't you be just a little more polite, Leo? I know you have no further use for me, but the least you can do is not treat me as though I'm something the cat dragged in.'

'Is it money?' His anger at himself for continuing to let her infiltrate his head and ambush his thoughts transferred into a healthy anger towards her and, although he knew he was being unfair, there was no way he was going to allow himself to be dragged down the apology route.

'I beg your pardon?'

'You know how rich I am now. You must know the lifestyle Bridget's enjoying—I'm sure she's told you so. Have you decided that you'd like me to throw some money in your direction for old times' sake?' God, was this *him*? He barely recognised the person behind the words.

Brianna clutched the phone so tightly that she thought she might break it in two. Did he know how insulting he was being right now? Did he care? How could she have misread someone so utterly? Was there some crazy missing connection in her head that allowed her to give everyone the benefit of the doubt, including people who were just bad for her health?

'You mentioned more than once that the place needed updating: new bar stools, new paint job on the outside, less tatty sofas in front of the fire…' The sofas had been damn near perfect, he seemed to recall. The sort of sofas a person could sink into and remain sunk in for hours, remain sunk in for a lifetime. 'Consider it done. On me. Call it thanks for, well, everything'

'How generous of you, Leo.' She reined in her explosive rage and kept her voice as neutral as she possibly could. 'And I suppose this might eventually have something to do with money. But I really need to see you face to face to talk about it.'

Perversely, Leo was disappointed that he had hit the nail on the head. Other women played the money angle. Other women assessed his wealth and expected a good time at his expense. It had never bothered him because, after all, fair's fair.

But Brianna… She wasn't like other women. Apparently, however, she was.

'Name the figure,' he said curtly.

'I'd rather not. If you could just make an appointment to see me. I could come to London and take the opportunity to look in on Bridget as well…'

'I have no free time during the day. I could see you tomorrow some time after six thirty, and I'm doing you a favour because that would involve cancelling a conference call.'

'Er…' Money she knew she didn't have disappeared through the window at the prospect of finding somewhere to stay, because there was no way she would be staying at his apartment, especially after she had dropped her bombshell.

'Take it or leave it.' He cut into her indecisive silence. 'I can meet you at seven at a bistro near my office.' He named it and then, from nowhere, pictured her sitting there at one of the tables, waiting for him. He pictured her face, her startling prettiness; he pictured her body, which would doubtless be concealed underneath something truly unappealing—that waterproof coat of hers of indeterminate green which she seemed to wear everywhere.

On cue, his body jerked into life, sourly reminding him of the way just thinking of her could manage to turn him on.

Tomorrow, he resolved, he would rifle through his address book and see whether there wasn't someone he could date, if only as a distraction. Bridget, oddly, had not referred back to that aborted conversation she had had with him at the pub, had made no mention of Brianna at all. She would think there was nothing amiss were he to start dating. In fact, she would think something was amiss if he *didn't*.

'Well?' he said impatiently. 'Will you be there? This is a going, going, gone situation.'

'I'll be there. See you tomorrow.'

Brianna barely slept through the night. She was having a baby! Unplanned, unexpected, but certainly not unwanted.

She was on edge as she finally landed on English soil. The weather had taken a turn for the better but, to be on the safe side, she had still decided to wear her faithful old coat just in case. The deeper into the city she got, the more ridiculously out of place she felt in her clothing. Even at nearly seven in the evening, the streets were packed. Everyone appeared to be dressed in suits, carrying briefcases and in a massive rush.

She had given the address of the bistro to the taxi driver but, when she was dropped off, she remained outside on the pavement, her battered pull-along in one hand, her other hand shoved into the capacious pocket of her coat. Nerves threatened to overwhelm her. In fact, she wanted nothing more than to hop into the nearest taxi and ask it to deliver her right back to the airport.

There were people coming and going from the bistro. She stood to one side, shaking like a leaf, aware of the pathetic figure she cut, and then she took a deep breath and entered with all the trepidation of someone entering a lion's den.

The noise was deafening, exaggerated by the starkness of the surroundings and the wooden floor. It was teeming with people, all young, all beautiful. A young woman clacking along in her high heels, with a leather case clutched to her side, tripped over her pull-along and swore profusely before giving her the once-over with contempt.

'Oh God, darling, are you lost? In case you haven't noticed, this isn't the bus station. If you and your luggage take a left out of the door and keep walking, you both should hit the nearest bus stop and they can deliver you wherever you're going.'

Brianna backed away, speechless, and looked around desperately for Leo. Right now, he felt like the only safe port in a storm and she spotted him tucked away towards the back of the room, sitting at a table and nursing a drink. A wave of relief washed over her as she began threading her way towards him, her pull-along bumping into ankles and calves and incurring a trail of oaths on the way.

Leo watched her zig-zag approach with brooding intensity. Amongst the city folk, snappily dressed and all braying in loud voices that competed to be heard, she was as natural and as beautiful as a wild flower. He couldn't fail to notice the sidelong looks she garnered from some of the men and he quickly knocked back the remainder of his whisky in one gulp.

So she had come here on her begging mission. He would have to do a bit better than stare at her and make favourable comparisons between her and the rest of the over-paid, over-confident, over-arrogant crowd on show. He signalled to a waiter to bring him another drink. It was a perk of this bar that he was the only one to receive waiter service, but then again, had it not been for his injection of cash years previously, the place would have been run into the ground. Now he owned a stake in it and, as soon as he clicked his fingers, the staff jumped to attention. It certainly saved the tedium of queuing at the bar trying to vie for attention. It also secured him the best table in the house, marginally away from the crowds.

'I'm sorry I'm a little late.' Brianna found that she could barely look at him without her entire nervous system gathering pace and going into overdrive. How had she managed to forget the impact he had on her senses? The way those dark, dark eyes could make her head swim and scramble her thoughts until she could barely speak?

'Sit.' He motioned to the chair facing him with a curt nod and she sank onto it and pulled her little bag alongside her. 'So…' He leant back and folded his arms. She was pink and her hair, which had obviously started the trip as a single braid down her back, was in the process of unravelling.

'I hadn't expected so much noise.' Her eyes skittered away from his face but then returned to look at him with resolve. She had to forget about being out of her depth. She had come here for one reason and one reason only and she wasn't going to let an attack of nerves stand in her way. How much more could he hurt her?

Leo cast a cursory glance around him and asked her what she wanted to drink: a glass of water. He would have expected something a little more stiff to get her through her 'begging bowl' speech, but to each their own. He ordered some mineral water and another stiff drink for himself then settled back with an air of palpable boredom.

Something in him railed against believing the worst of her, knowing her to be the person that she was, yet he refused to give house room to that voice. He felt he needed to be black and white or else forever be lost. Let it not be forgotten that she had refused to listen to him when he had attempted to explain the reason for his fabrications. She had turned her back and stalked off and for the past month he had seen and heard nothing from her.

She had taken off her coat, the gruesome coat which he was annoyed to discover made inroads into his indifference, because he could remember teasing her that she needed something a little less worn, that waterproof coats like that were never fashion statements.

'What's it like?' Brianna opened the conversation with something as far removed from what she actually needed to say as she could get, and Leo shot her a perplexed glance.

'What's what like? What are you talking about?'

'Having your... Having Bridget in your life. It must be very satisfying for you.'

Leo flushed. No one knew about Bridget, aside from Harry. He had never been the sort of man who spilled his guts to all and sundry and there had been absolutely no temptation to tell anyone about his mother living with him. He had not been dating, so there had been no women coming to his apartment, asking questions. Even if there had been, it was debatable whether he would have confided in any of them or not. He looked at her open, upturned face and found it hard to resurrect his cynicism.

'It's working for me,' he said gruffly. Working for them both. The years had dropped off his mother. She had been to the hairdresser, had her hair styled, had her nails done... She bore little resemblance to the fragile creature he had first set eyes on.

Drinks were brought and he sat back to allow the waiter to fuss as he put them on the table, along with a plate of appetisers which had not been ordered. 'But you didn't come here to talk about my relationship with Bridget.'

'No, I didn't, but I'm interested.' She just couldn't launch into her real reason for coming to London without some sort of preamble.

And, an inner voice whispered, didn't she just want to prolong being in his company, like a thief stealing time that didn't belong to them? Didn't she just want to breathe him in, that clean, masculine scent, and slide her eyes over a body she knew so well even when, as now, it was sheathed in the finest tailored suit money could buy?

'Just tell me why you're here, Brianna. You said something about money. How much are you looking for?'

'It's a bit more complicated than that.'

'What's more complicated than asking for a hand-out?'

Brianna looked down and fiddled with the bottle of water before pouring a little more into her glass. She envied him his stiff drink. She felt that under different circumstances, without this baby inside her, she could have done with a little Dutch courage.

'Leo…' She looked him directly in the eye and felt that this was the last time that she would be seeing him like this: a free man who could do whatever he wanted to do. She could even appreciate that, however dismissive he was of her now, it was an emotion that would soon be overtaken by far more overwhelming ones. Perhaps, thinking about it, it was just as well that they were having this conversation somewhere noisy and crowded.

'I'm pregnant.'

For a few seconds, Leo thought that he might have misheard her, but even as his mind was absorbing her body language—taking in the way she now couldn't meet his eyes, the hectic flush on her cheeks, the way her hand was trembling on the glass—he still couldn't put two and two together.

'Come again?' He leaned forward, straining to catch her every word. There was a buzzing in his ears that was growing louder by the second.

'I'm having a baby, Leo. Your baby. I'm sorry. I do realise that this is probably the last thing in the world you expected to hear, and the last thing you *wanted* to hear, but I felt you ought to know. I did think about keeping it to myself but that would have been impossible. Well, you know how small the place is, and sooner or later Bridget would have found out. In fact, there's no way that I would have wanted to keep it from her.'

Why wasn't he saying anything? She had expected more of an immediate and explosive reaction, but then he was probably still in a state of shock.

'You're telling me that you're having my baby.' The words felt odd as they passed his lips. The thought had taken root now with blinding clarity and he looked down at her stomach. She was as slender as she had always been. He heard himself asking questions: how pregnant was she? Was she absolutely certain? Had it been verified by a doctor? He knew home tests existed but any test that could be done at home would always be open to error…

'I'm not expecting anything from you,' Brianna ended. 'I just thought that you ought to know.'

'You thought that *I ought to know*?' Leo shot her a look of utter incredulity. The impersonal bistro he had chosen now seemed inappropriate. Restless energy was pouring through his body and, as fast as he tried to decipher a pattern to what he was thinking, his thoughts came unstuck, leaving him with just the explosive realisation that in a matter of months he was going to be a father.

'I realise that you might want to have some input…'

'You have got to be kidding me, Brianna. You come here, drop this bombshell on me, and the only two things you can find to say are that you felt I *ought to know* and you realise that I *might want some input*? We have to get out of here.'

'And go where?' she cried.

'Somewhere a little less *full of chattering morons.*'

'I'm not going to your apartment,' she said, refusing to budge and clutching the sides of her chair as though fearful that at any moment he might just get it into his head to bodily pick her up and haul her over his shoulder to the front door, caveman style.

'I haven't said anything to Bridget yet and I'd rather not just at the moment. I…I need time to absorb it all myself so, if you don't mind, I'd quite like to stay here. Not that there's much more for me to bring to the table.'

'And another classic line from you. God, I just don't believe this.'

Brianna watched as he dropped his head to

his hands. 'I'm so sorry to be the bearer of un-expected tidings. Like I said, though…'

'Spare me whatever pearls of wisdom are going to emerge from your mouth, Brianna.' He raised his head to stare at her. 'It is as it is, and now we're going to have to decide how we deal with this situation.' He rubbed his eyes and continued holding her gaze with his.

'Perhaps you should go away and think about this. It's a lot to take on board. We could fix a time to meet again.'

'I don't think so.' He straightened and sat back. 'Waiting for another day isn't going to alter this problem.'

Brianna stiffened. 'This isn't your problem, it's mine, and I don't see it as a *problem*. I'm going to be the one having the baby and I shall be the one looking after it. I recognise that you'll want to contribute in some way, but let me assure you that I expect nothing from you.'

'Do you honestly believe that you can dump this on me and I'm going to walk away from it?'

'I don't know. A few weeks ago I would have said that the guy at the pub who helped clear snow wouldn't, but then you weren't that guy at all, were you? So, honestly? I have no idea.' She sat on her hands and leaned towards him. 'If you want to contribute financially, then that would be fine and much appreciated. I don't expect you to give anything to me, but helping to meet the needs of the baby would be okay. They may be small, but they can be very expensive, and you know all too well what the finances at the pub are like. Especially with all the closures of late.'

'I know what you think of me, Brianna, but I'm not a man to run away from my responsibilities—and in this instance my responsibilities don't stop at sending you a monthly cheque to cover baby food.'

'They don't?' Brianna queried uneasily. She wondered what else he had in mind. 'Naturally you would be free to see your child whenever you wanted, but it might be difficult, considering you live in London…' She quailed inwardly at the prospect of him turning up at the front door. She wondered whether the onslaught of times remembered, before she had discovered who he really was, would be just too much for her. Not that she would have any choice. It would be his right to visit his child, whether it made her uncomfortable or not.

'Visiting rights? No, I don't think so.'

'I won't let you take custody of my baby.'

'*Our* baby,' he corrected.

Brianna blanched as her worst imaginings went into free fall. She hadn't even thought that he might want to take the baby away from her, yet, why hadn't that occurred to her? He was adopted. He would have very strong feelings about being on hand as a father because his own real father had not been on hand. And, whatever concoctions he had come up with to disguise his true identity, she knew instinctively that he possessed a core of inner integrity.

And those concoctions, she was reluctantly forced to conclude, had not been fabricated for the sheer hell of it. They had been done for a reason and, once he had embarked on that road, it would have been difficult to get off it.

Would that core of integrity propel him to try and fight her for custody of the baby? He was rolling in money whilst she was borderline broke and, when it came to getting results, the guy who was rolling in money was always going to win hands down over the woman who was borderline broke. You didn't need a degree in quantum physics to work that one out.

'You can stop looking as though you're about to pass out, Brianna. I have no intention of indulging in a protracted battle with you to take custody of our baby.' He was slightly surprised at how naturally the words 'our baby' rolled off his tongue. The shock appeared to have worn off far more quickly than might have been expected, but then he prided himself as being the sort of guy who could roll with the punches and come up with solutions in the tightest of spots.

Brianna breathed a sigh of relief. 'So what are you proposing?'

'We get married. Obvious solution.'

'You have got to be joking.'

'Do I look like someone about to burst into laughter?'

'That's a crazy idea.'

'Explain why.'

'Because it's not a solution, Leo. Two people don't just *get married* because, accidentally, there's a baby on the way. Two people who *broke up.* Two people who wouldn't have laid eyes on one another again were it not for the fact that the girl in question happens to find herself pregnant.'

'Brianna, I'm not prepared to take a backseat in the upbringing of my child. I'm not prepared for any child of mine to ever think that they got less of me than they might have wanted.'

'I'm not asking you to take a back seat in anything.'

'Nor,' Leo continued, overriding her interruption as though it hadn't registered, 'am I willing to watch on the sidelines as you find yourself another man who decides to take over the upbringing of my child.'

'That's not likely to happen! I think I've had enough of men to last a lifetime.'

'Of course, you'll have to move to London, but in all events that won't depend on the sale of the pub. In fact, you can hand it over to someone else to run on your behalf.'

'Are you listening to a *word* I'm saying?'

'Are you listening to what *I'm* saying?' he said softly. 'I hope so, because the proposal I've put on the table is the only solution at hand.'

'This isn't a maths problem that needs a solution. This is something completely different.'

'I'm failing to see your objections, aside from a selfish need to put yourself ahead of our child.'

'I could never live in London. And I could never marry someone for the wrong reasons. We would end up resenting one another and that would be the worst possible atmosphere in which to raise a child. Don't you see that?'

'Before you knew who I was,' Leo said tautly, his dark eyes fixed intently on her face, 'did you hope that our relationship would go further?'

He sat forward and all of a sudden her space was invaded and she could barely breathe. 'I knew that you weren't intending on hanging around,' she said and she could hear the choked breathlessness in her voice. 'You said so. You made that perfectly clear.'

'Which doesn't answer my question. Were you hoping for more?'

'I didn't think it would end the way it did,' she threw back at him with bristling defiance.

'But it did, and you may not have liked the

way it ended, but what we had…' He watched the slow colour creep up her cheeks and a rush of satisfaction poured through him, because behind those lowered eyes he could *smell* the impact he still had on her.

'This wouldn't be a marriage in name only for the sake of a child. This would be a marriage in every sense of the word because—let's not kid each other—what we had was good.' Her naked, pale body flashed through his mind, as did the memory of all those little whimpering noises she made when he touched her, the way her nostrils flared and her eyelids quivered as her body gathered pace and hurtled towards orgasm. He already felt himself harden at the thought and this time he didn't try to kill it at source because it was inappropriate given she was no longer part of his life. She was a part of his life now, once again, and the freedom to think of her without restraint was a powerful kick to his system.

'What we had was…was…'

'Was good and you know it. Shall I remind you how good it was?' He didn't give her time to move or time even to think about what was coming. He leant across the small table, cupped his hand on the nape of her neck and pulled her towards him.

Brianna's body responded with the knee-jerk response of immediate reaction, as though responding with learned behaviour. Her mouth parted and the feel his tongue thrusting against her was as heady as the most powerful drug. Her mind emptied and she kissed him back, and she felt as though she never wanted the kiss to end. The coolness of his withdrawal, leaving her with her mouth still slightly parted and her eyes half-closed, was a horrifying return to reality.

'Point proven,' he murmured softly. 'So, when I tell you that you need to look outside the box and start seeing the upsides to my proposal, you know what I'm talking about. This won't be a union without one or two definite bonuses.'

'I'll never move to London and I'll never marry you.' Her breathing was only now returning to normal and the mortification of what she had done, of how her treacherous body had *betrayed* her, felt like acid running through her veins. 'I'm going now but I'll give you a call in a couple of days. When you're ready to accept what I've said, then we'll talk again.' She stood up on wobbly legs and turned her back. The urge to run away as fast as she could was overpowering, and she did. Out to the pavement, where she hailed the nearest taxi and instructed him to drive her to a hotel—something cheap, something close to the airport.

She wouldn't marry him. He didn't love her and there was no way that she would ever accept sacrificing both their lives for the wrong reason, whatever he said about the bonus of good sex. Good sex would die and then where would they be?

But she had to get away because she knew that there was something craven and weak in the very deepest part of her that might *just* play with the idea.

And there was no way she was going to give that weak, craven part of her a voice.

CHAPTER NINE

LEO LOOKED AT the sprawling house facing him and immediately wondered whether he had gone for the wrong thing. Too big, maybe? Too ostentatious? Too much land?

He shook his head with frustration and fired a couple of questions at the estate agent without bothering to glance in her direction.

In the space of six weeks, this was the eighth property he had personally seen out in the rolling Berkshire countryside, sufficiently far away from London to promote the idea of clean air, whilst being within easy commuting distance from the city.

Brianna had no idea that he was even hunting down a house. As far as she was concerned, he was the guy she'd refused to commit to who seemed intent on pursuing her even though she had already given him her answer—again and again and again, in varying formats, but all conveying the same message.

No thank you, I won't be getting married to you.

On the upside, he had managed to persuade her temporarily to move to London, although that in itself had been a task of no small order. She had refused to budge, had informed him that he was wasting his time, that they weren't living in the Victorian ages. She had folded her arms, given him a gimlet stare of pure stubbornness. He had been reduced to deviating from his intention to get what he wanted—what was *needed*, at all costs—in favour of thinking creatively.

For starters, he had had to pursue her to Ireland because she'd refused to continue her conversation with him in London. And then, he had had to travel to the pub to see her, because she didn't want him staying under her roof, not given the circumstances. He had refrained from pointing out the saying about horses bolting and stable doors. He had initiated his process of getting what he wanted by pointing out that it made sense.

He had done that over the finest meal to be had in a really very good restaurant not a million miles away from the pub. He had used every argument in the book and had got precisely nowhere. Then he had returned, this time to try and persuade her to see his point of view during a bracing walk by one of the lakes with the wind whipping his hair into disarray and his mega-expensive coat proving no match for the cold. He had tried to remind her of the sexual chemistry that was still there between them, but had cut short that line of argument when she'd threatened to walk back to the pub without him.

He had informed her that there wasn't a single woman alive who wouldn't have chewed off his arm to accept an offer of marriage from him, which had been another tactical error.

He had dropped all talk of anything and concentrated on just making her feel comfortable in his presence, whilst marvelling that she could carry on keeping him at arm's length, considering how close they had been. But by this point he had been clued up enough to make sure that he didn't hark back to the past. Nothing to remind her about how much she clearly loathed him, having found out about his lies.

Never in his life had Leo put this much effort into one woman.

And never in his life had he had so many cold showers. From having given no thought whatsoever to settling down, far less having a child, he now seemed fixated by the baby growing inside her and, the more fixated he became, the more determined he was that she would marry him. He was turned on by everything about her. Turned on by the way she moved, the way she looked at him, by all her little gestures that seemed ingrained inside his head so that, even when she wasn't around, he was thinking about her constantly.

Was it a case of the inaccessible becoming more and more desirable? Was it because she was now carrying his baby that his body seemed to be on fire for her all the time? Or was it just that he hadn't stopped wanting her because it had been a highly physical relationship that had not been given the opportunity of dying a natural death?

He didn't know and he didn't bother analysing it. He just knew that he still wanted her more than he could remember wanting anyone. He wanted her to be his. The thought of some other man stepping into his shoes, doing clever things behind the bar of the pub and having a say in his child's welfare, made him grit his teeth together in impotent rage.

The estate agent, a simpering woman in her thirties, was saying something about the number of bedrooms and Leo scowled.

'How many?'

'Eight! Perfect for having the family over!'

'Too many. And I can look at it from here and see straight away that it would be far too big for the person I have in mind.'

'Perhaps the lucky lady would like to pop along and have a look for herself? It's really rather grand inside…'

Leo flinched at the word 'grand'. He pictured Brianna wiping the bar with a cloth, standing back in her old jeans and sloppy jumper to survey her handiwork, before retiring to the comfy sofa in the lounge which had been with her practically since she'd been a kid. She wouldn't have a clue what to do with 'grand' and he had a gut feeling that if he settled on anything like this she would end up blaming him.

How, he thought as house number nine bit the dust, had he managed to end up with the one woman in the world to whom a marriage proposal was an insult and who was determined to fight him every inch of the way? Even though the air sizzled between them with a raw, elemental electricity that neither of them could deny.

But at least he had managed to get her to London. It was a comforting thought as his Ferrari ate up the miles back to the city centre and his penthouse apartment.

He had appealed to her sense of fairness. He wanted to be there while she was pregnant and what better way than for her to move to London? No need to live in his apartment. He would find somewhere else for her, somewhere less central. It would be great for Bridget as well. Indeed, it would be a blessing in disguise, for Bridget was tiring of the concrete jungle of inner London. She was back on her feet, albeit in a restricted way,

220   SECRETS OF A RUTHLESS TYCOON

and the constant crowds terrified her. They could
share something small but cosy in West London.
He would personally see to it that a manager was
located for the pub…

She had acquiesced. That had been ten days
ago and, although he had made sure to visit them
both every evening after work, he had ostensibly
dropped all mention of marriage.

That aggressive need to conquer had been
forced into retreat and he was now playing a
waiting game. He wasn't sure what would happen if that waiting game didn't work and he pre-
ferred not to dwell on that. Instead, he phoned his
secretary and found out what other gems were
available on the property market in picturesque
Berkshire.

'Too impressive,' he told her about his last
failed viewing. It was added to all the other too
'something or other' that had characterised the
last eight viewings, all of which had come to
nothing. He laughed when she suggested that he
send someone in his place to at least narrow the
possibilities.

He couldn't imagine anyone he knew having
the slightest idea as to what to look for when it
came to Brianna. They were people who only
knew a London crowd, socialites for whom there
could be nothing that could ever be too grand.

'Find me some more properties.' He concluded

his conversation with his long-suffering PA. 'And forget about the marble bathrooms and indoor swimming pools. Go smaller.'

He hung up. It wasn't yet two-thirty in the afternoon. He had never taken this much time off work in his life before. Except for when he had voluntarily marooned himself at Brianna's pub. And yet, he was driven to continue his search. Work, meetings and deals would just have to take a back seat.

His secretary called him on his mobile just as he was leaving the M25, heading into London.

'It's a small village near, er, Sunningdale. Er, shall I read you the details? It's just on the market. Today, in fact. Thank goodness for estate agents who remember we exist…'

Leo thought that most estate agents would remember any client for whom money was no object. 'I'll check that out now.' He was already halfway back to London but he manoeuvred his car off the motorway and back out. 'Cancel my five o'clock meeting.'

'You've already cancelled Sir Hawkes twice.'

'In that case, let Reynolds cover. He's paid enough; a little delegation in his direction will do him the world of good.'

He made it to the small village in good time and, the very second he saw the picture-postcard cottage with the sprawling garden in the back and the white picket fence at the front, he knew he had hit the jackpot.

He didn't bother with an offer. He would pay the full asking price and came with cash in hand. The estate agent couldn't believe his luck. Leo waved aside the man's ingratiating and frankly irritating bowing and scraping and elicited all the pertinent details he needed for an immediate purchase.

'And if the occupants need time to find somewhere else, you can tell them that they'll be generously compensated over and beyond what they want for the house to leave immediately.' He named a figure and the estate agent practically swooned. 'Here's my card. Call me in an hour and we'll get the ball rolling. Oh, and I'll be bringing someone round tomorrow, if not sooner, to look at it. Make sure it's available.' He was at his car and the rotund estate agent was dithering behind him, clutching the business card as though it were a gold ingot.

'What if…?' He cleared his throat anxiously as he was forced to contemplate a possible hitch in clinching his commission. 'What if the sellers want to wait and see if a better offer comes along?'

About to slide into the driving seat, Leo paused and looked at the much shorter man with a wry expression. 'Oh, trust me, that won't be happening.'

'Sir…'

'Call me——and I'll be expecting a conversation that I want to hear.' He left the man staring at him red-faced, perspiring and doubtless contemplating the sickening prospect of sellers who might prove too greedy to accept the quick sale.

Leo knew better. They simply wouldn't be able to believe their luck.

He could easily have made it back to the office to catch the tail end of the meeting he had cancelled at the last minute. Instead, he headed directly to Brianna's house, which was an effortless drive off the motorway and into London suburbia.

Brianna heard the low growl of the Ferrari as it pulled up outside the house. It seemed her ears were attuned to the sound. She immediately schooled her expression into one of polite aloofness. In the kitchen Bridget was making them both a cup of tea, fussing as she always seemed to do now, clucking around her like a mother hen because she was pregnant, even though Brianna constantly told her that pregnancy wasn't an illness and that Bridget was the one in need of looking after.

'He's early this evening!' Bridget exclaimed with pleasure. 'I wonder why? I think I'll give

you two a little time together and have a nice,
long bath. The doctor says that I should take it
easy. You know that.'

Brianna raised her eyebrows wryly and stood
up. 'I don't think chatting counts as not taking it
easy,' she pointed out. 'Besides, you know Leo
enjoys seeing you when he gets here.' Every time
she saw them together, she felt a lump of emotion gather at the back of her throat. However
cut-throat and ruthless he might be, and however much of a lying bastard he had been, he was
always gentle with Bridget. He didn't call her
'Mum' but he treated her with the respect and
consideration any mother would expect from her
child. And they spoke of all the inconsequential
things that happened on a daily basis. Perhaps
they had explored the past already and neither
wanted to revisit it.

At any rate, Bridget was a changed person.
She looked healthier, more *vibrant*. The sort of
woman who was actually only middle-aged, who
could easily get out there and find herself another guy but who seemed perfectly content to
age gracefully by herself.

She quelled the urge to insist to Bridget that
she stay put as the older woman began heading to
her bedroom on the ground floor—a timely co-
incidence because the owners of the house from

whom they were renting had had to cater for an ageing relative of their own.

Her stomach clenched as she heard the key being inserted into the front door.

She still wondered how he had managed to talk her into moving to London, a city she hated because it was too fast, too crowded and too noisy for her tastes.

But move to London she had, admittedly to a quieter part of the city, and now that she was here she was in danger of becoming just a little too accustomed to having Leo around. Okay, so he didn't show up *every* evening, and he never stayed the night, but his presence was becoming an addiction she knew she ought to fight.

He had dropped all talk of marriage and yet she still felt on red alert the second he walked through the door. Her eyes still feasted surreptitiously on him and, even though she knew that she should be thanking her lucky stars that he was no longer pursuing the whole marriage thing— because he had 'come to his senses' and 'seen the foolishness of hitching his wagon to a woman he didn't love'—she was oddly deflated by the ease with which he had jettisoned the subject.

As always, her first sight of him as he strode into the small hallway, with its charming flagstone floor and tiny stained-glass window to one side, was one of intense *awareness*. She literally felt her mouth go dry.

'You're here earlier than…um…normal.' She watched as he dealt her a slashing smile, one that made her legs go to jelly, one that made her want to hurl herself at him and wrap her arms around his neck. Every time she felt like this, she recalled what he had said about any marriage between them having upsides, having the distinct bonus of very good sex…

Leo's eyes swept over her in an appraisal that was almost unconscious. He took in the loose trousers, because there was just a hint of a stomach beginning to show; the baggy clothes that would have rendered any woman drab and unappealing but which seemed unbelievably sexy when she was wearing them.

'Is Bridget around?' He had to drag his eyes away from her. Hell, she had told him in no uncertain terms that mutual sexual attraction just wasn't enough on which to base a marriage, so how was it that she still turned him on? Even more so, now that she was carrying his baby.

'She's upstairs resting.'

'There's something I want to show you.' He had no doubt that he would be able to view the property at this hour. He was, after all, in the driving seat. 'So…why don't you get your coat on? It's a drive away.'

'What do you want to show me?'

'It's a surprise.'

'You know I hate surprises.' She blushed when he raised one eyebrow, amused at that titbit of shared confidence between them.

'This won't be the sort of surprise you got two years ago when you returned from a weekend away to find the pub flooded.'

'I'm not dressed for a meal out.' Nor was she equipped for him to resume his erosion of her defences and produce more arguments for having his way…although she killed the little thrill at the prospect of having him try and convince her to marry him.

'You look absolutely fine.' He looked her over with a thoroughness that brought hectic colour to her cheeks. And, while he disappeared to have a few quick words with Bridget, Brianna took the opportunity—cursing herself, because why on earth did it matter, really?—to dab on a little bit of make-up and do something with her hair. She also took off the sloppy clothes and, although her jeans were no longer a perfect fit, she extracted the roomiest of them from the wardrobe and twinned them with a brightly coloured thick jumper that at least did flattering things for her complexion.

'So, where are we going?' They had cleared

some of the traffic and were heading out towards the motorway. 'Why are we leaving London?'

Leo thought of the perfect cottage nestled in the perfect grounds with all those perfect features and his face relaxed into a smile. 'And you're smiling.' For some reason that crooked half-smile disarmed her. Here in the car, as they swept out of London on a remarkably fine afternoon, she felt infected with a holiday spirit, a reaction to the stress she had been under for the past few weeks. 'A man's allowed to smile, isn't he?' He flashed her a sideways glance that warmed her face. 'We're having a baby, Brianna. Being cold towards one another is not an option.'

Except, she thought, *he* hadn't been cold towards *her*. He had done his damnedest to engage her in conversation and, thus far, he had remained undeterred by her lack of enthusiasm for engagement. She chatted because Bridget was usually there with them and he, annoyingly, ignored her cagey responses and acted as though everything was perfectly fine between them. He cheerfully indulged his mother's obvious delight in the situation and, although neither of them had mentioned the marriage proposal, they both knew that Bridget was contemplating that outcome with barely contained glee.

'I hadn't realised that I was being cold,' she said stiffly. Her eyes drifted to his strong forearms on the steering wheel. He had tossed his jacket in the back seat and rolled up the sleeves of his shirt to his elbows. She couldn't look even at that slither of bare skin, the sprinkling of dark hair on his arms, without her mind racing backwards in time to when they were lovers and those hands were exploring every inch of her body.

'No, sometimes you're not,' he murmured in a low voice and Brianna looked at him narrowly.

'Meaning?'

'Meaning that there are many times when your voice is cool but the glances you give me are anything but...' He switched the radio on to soft classical music, leaving her to ponder that remark in silence. Did he expect her to say something in answer to that? And what could she say? She *knew* that he had an effect on her; she *knew* that she just couldn't stop herself from sliding those sidelong glances at him, absorbing the way he moved, the curve of his mouth, the lazy dark eyes. Of course he would have noticed! What *didn't* he notice?

She was so wrapped up in her thoughts that she only noticed that they had completely left London behind when fields, scattered villages and towns replaced the hard strip of the motorway, and then she turned to him with confusion.

'We're in the countryside.' She frowned and then her breath caught in her throat as he glanced across to her with amusement.

'Well spotted.'

'It's a bit far to go for a meal out.' Perhaps he wanted to talk to her about something big, something important. Maybe he was going to tell her that he had listened to everything she had said and had come to the conclusion that he could survive with her returning to Ireland whilst he popped up occasionally to see his offspring. Perhaps he thought that a destination far away would be suitable for that kind of conversation, because it would allow her time to absorb it on the return trip back into London.

Had having her at close quarters reminded him of how little he wanted any kind of committed relationship? Had familiarity bred the proverbial contempt? For maybe the first time in his life, he had been tied to a routine of having to curtail his work life to accommodate both her and Bridget. Had he seen that as a dire warning of what might be expected should he pursue his intention of marrying her, and had it put him off?

The more she thought about it, the more convinced she was that whatever he had to say over a charming pub dinner in the middle of nowhere would be...

Something she wouldn't want to hear.

Yet she knew that that was the wrong reaction. She needed to be strong and determined in the road she wanted to follow. She didn't want a half-baked marriage with a guy who felt himself trapped, for whom the only option looming was to saddle himself with her for the rest of his life. No way!

But her heart was beating fast and there was a ball of misery unfurling inside her with each passing signpost.

When the car turned off the deserted road, heading up a charming avenue bordered by trees not yet in leaf, she lay back and half-closed her eyes.

She opened them as they drew up outside one of the prettiest houses she had ever seen.

'Where are we?'

'This is what I wanted to show you.' Leo could barely contain the satisfaction in his voice. He had been sold on first sight. On second sight, he was pleased to find that there was no let-down. It practically had her name written all over it.

'You wanted to show me a *house*?'

'Come on.' He swung out of the car and circled round to hold her door open for her, resisting the urge to help her out, because she had already told him that she hadn't suddenly morphed into a piece of delicate china simply because she was pregnant.

Brianna dawdled behind him as he strode towards the front door and stooped to recover a key which had been placed underneath one of the flower pots at the side of the front step. What the hell was going on? She took a deep breath and realised that, although they were only a matter of forty-five minutes out of West London, the air smelled different. Cleaner.

'This isn't just any house.' He turned to look at her and was pleased at the expression on her face, which was one of rapt appreciation. 'Bar the technicalities, I've bought this house.'

'You've *bought* this house?'

'Come in and tell me what you think.'

'But…'

'Shh…' He placed a finger gently over her parted lips and the feel of his warm skin against hers made her tremble. 'You can ask all the questions you want after you've had a look around.'

Despite the fact that he had only looked around the place once, Leo had no hesitation on acting as tour guide for the house, particularly pointing out all the quaint features he was certain she would find delightful. There was a real fire in both the sitting room and the snug, an Aga in the kitchen, bottle-green bedrooms that overlooked an orchard, which he hadn't actually noticed on first viewing, but which he now felt qualified to show her with some pride. He watched as she dawdled in the rooms, staring out of the windows, touching the curtains and trailing her finger along the polished oak banister as they returned downstairs, ending up in the kitchen, which had a splendid view of the extensive back gardens.

The owners had clearly been as bowled over by his over-the-top, generous offer as he had anticipated. There was a bottle of champagne on the central island and two champagne glasses.

'Well? What do you think?'

'It's wonderful,' Brianna murmured. 'I'd never have thought that you could find somewhere like this so close to London. Is it going to be a second home for you?'

'It's going to be a first home for us.'

Brianna felt as though the breath had temporarily been knocked out of her. Elation zipped through her at the thought of this—a house, the perfect house, shared with the man she loved and their child. In the space of a few seconds, she projected into the future where she saw their son or daughter enjoying the open space, running through the garden with a dog trailing behind, while she watched from the kitchen window with Leo right there behind her, sitting by the big pine table, chatting about his day.

The illusion disappeared almost as fast as it had surfaced because that was never going to be reality. The reality would be her, stuck out here on her own, while Leo carried on working all hours in the city, eventually bored by the woman he was stuck with. He would do his duty for his child but the image of cosy domesticity was an illusion and she had to face that.

'It's not going to work,' she said abruptly, turning away and blinking back stupid tears. 'Nothing's changed, Leo, and you can't bribe me into marrying you with a nice house and a nice garden.'

For a few seconds, Leo wasn't sure that he had heard her correctly. He had been so confident of winning her over with the house that he was lost for words as what she had said gradually sank in.

'I didn't realise that I was trying to bribe you,' he muttered in a driven undertone. He raked his fingers through his hair and grappled with an inability to get his thoughts in order. 'You liked the house; you said so.'

'I do, but a house isn't enough, just like sex isn't enough. That glue would never keep us together.' The words felt as though they had been ripped out of her and she had to turn away because she just couldn't bear to see his face.

'Right.' And still he couldn't quite get it through his head that she had turned him down, that any notion of marriage was over. He hesitated and stared at the stubborn angle of her profile then he strode towards the door. He was filled with a surge of restlessness, a keen desire to be outside, as if the open air might clear his head and point him towards a suitably logical way forward.

It was a mild evening and he circled the house, barely taking in the glorious scenery he had earlier made a great show of pointing out to her.

Inside, Brianna heard the slam of the front door and spun around, shaking like a leaf. The void he had left behind felt like a physical, tangible weight in the room, filling it up until she thought she would suffocate.

Where had he gone? Surely he wouldn't just drive off and leave her alone here in the middle of nowhere? She contemplated the awkward drive back into London and wondered whether it wouldn't be better to be stuck out here. But, when she dashed out of the front door, it was to find his car parked exactly where it had been when they had first arrived. And he was nowhere to be seen.

He was a grown man, fully capable of taking care of himself, and yet as she dashed down the drive to the main road and peered up and down, failing to spot him, she couldn't stop a surge of panic rising inside her.

What if he had been run over by a car? It was very quiet here, she sternly told herself; what called itself the main road was hardly a thoroughfare. . In fact, no more than a tractor or two and the occasional passing car, so there was no need to get into a flap. But, like a runaway train, she saw in her mind's eyes his crumpled body lying at the kerbside, and she felt giddy and nauseous at the thought of it.

She circled the house at a trot, circled it again and then…she saw him sitting on the ground under one of the trees, his back towards the house. Sitting on the *muddy* ground in his hand-tailored Italian suit.

'What are you doing?' She approached him cautiously because for the life of her she had never seen him like this—silent, his head lowered, his body language so redolent of vulnerability that she felt her breath catch painfully in her throat.

He looked up at her and her mouth went dry. 'You have no intention of ever forgiving me for the lie I told you, have you?' he asked so quietly that she had to bend a little to hear what he was saying. 'Even though you know that I had no intention of engineering a lie when I first arrived. Even though you know, or you *should* know, that what appeared harmless to me at the time was simply a means towards an end. I was thinking on my feet. I never expected to end up painting myself into the box of pathological liar.'

'I know you're not that,' Brianna said tentatively. She settled on the ground next to him. 'Your suit's going to be ruined.'

'So will your jeans.'

'My jeans cost considerably less than your suit.' She ventured a small smile and met with nothing in response, just those dark, dark eyes boring into her. More than anything else she wanted to bridge the small gap between them and reach for his hand, hold it in hers, but she knew that that was just love, her love for him, and it wouldn't change anything. She had to stand firm, however tough it was. She had to project ahead and not listen to the little voice in her head telling her that his gesture, his magnificent gesture of buying this perfect house for her, was a sign of something more significant.

'You were right,' he admitted in the same sort of careful voice that was so disconcerting.

'Right about what?'

'I was trying to bribe you with this house. The garden. Anything that would induce you to give us a chance. But nothing will ever be enough for you to do that because you can't forgive me for my deception, even though it was a deception that was never intended to hurt you.'

'I felt like I didn't know who you were, Leo,' Brianna said quietly. 'One minute you were the man helping out at the pub, mucking in, presumably writing your book when you were closeted away in the corner of the bar…and then the next minute you're some high-flying millionaire with a penthouse apartment and a bunch of companies, and the book you were writing was never a book at all. It was just loads of work and emails so that you could keep your businesses ticking over while you stayed at the pub and used me to get information about Bridget.'

'God, Brianna it wasn't like that…' But she had spelt out the basic facts and strung them together in a way that made sense, yet made no sense whatsoever. He felt like a man with one foot off the edge of a precipice he hadn't even known existed. All his years of control, of always being able to manage whatever situation was thrown at him, evaporated, replaced by a confusing surge of emotions that rushed through him like a tsunami.

He pressed his thumbs against his eyes and fought off the craven urge to cry. Hell, he hadn't cried since his father had died!

'But it was,' she said gently. 'And even if I did forgive you…' *and she had* '…the ingredients for a good marriage just aren't there.'

'For you, maybe' He raised his head to stare solemnly at her. 'But for me, the ingredients are all there.'

CHAPTER TEN

HE LOOKED AT her solemnly and then looked away, not because he couldn't hold her stare, but because he was afraid of what he might see there, a decision made, a mind closed off to what he had to say.

'When I came to search out my mother, I had already presumed to know what sort of person she was: irresponsible, a lowlife, someone without any kind of moral code… In retrospect, it was a facile assumption, but still it was the assumption I had already made.'

'Then why on earth did you bother coming?'

'Curiosity,' Leo said heavily. Rarely given to long explanations for his behaviour, he knew that he had to take his time now and, funnily enough, talking to her was easy. But then, he had talked to her, really talked to her, a lot more than he had ever talked to any other woman in his life before. That should have been a clue to the direction his heart was taking, but it had been a clue he had failed to pick up on.

Now he had a painful, desperate feeling that everything he should have said had been left too late. In his whole life, he had never taken his eye off the ball, had never missed connections. He had got where he had not simply because he was incredibly smart and incredibly proactive but because he could read situations with the same ease with which he could read people. He always knew when to strike and when to hold back.

That talent seemed to have deserted him now. He felt that if he said one wrong word she would take flight, and then where would he be?

'I had a wonderful upbringing, exemplary, but there was always something at the back of my mind, something that needed to fill in the missing blanks.'

'I can get that.'

'I always assumed that…' He inhaled deeply and then sat back with his eyes closed. This was definitely not the best spot to be having this conversation but somehow it felt right, being outside with her. She was such an incredibly outdoors person.

'That?'

'That there must be something in me that ruled my emotions. My adoptive parents were very much in love. I had the best example anyone could have had of two people who actually made the institution of marriage work for them. And yet, commitment was something I had always instinctively rejected. At the back of my mind, I wondered whether this had something to do with the fact that I was adopted; maybe being given away as a baby had left a lasting legacy of imper- manence, or maybe it was just some rogue gene that had found its way into my bloodstream; some crazy connection to the woman who gave birth to me, something that couldn't be eradicated.'

Brianna let the conversation wander. She wanted to reassure him that no such rogue gene existed in anyone, that whatever reasons he might have had in the past for not committing it was entirely within his power to alter that.

Except, she didn't want him to leap to the con- clusion that any altering should be done on her behalf. She was still clinging to a thread of com- mon sense that was telling her not to drop all her defences because he seemed so vulnerable. He might be one-hundred per cent sincere in wanting her to marry him, but without the right emotions she would have to stick fast to her decision. But it was difficult when her heart wanted to reach out to him and just assure him that she would do whatever it took to smooth that agonised expres- sion from his face.

'As you know, I've been biding my time until I made this trip to find her. I had always prom- ised myself that hunting down my past would be something I would do when my parents were no longer around.'

'I'm surprised you could have held out so long,' Brianna murmured. 'I would have wanted to find out straight away.'

'But then that's only one big difference between us, isn't it?' He gave her a half-smile that made her toes curl and threatened to permanently dislodge that fragile thread of common sense to which she was clinging for dear life. 'And I didn't appreciate just how *good* those differences between us were.'

'Really?' Brianna asked breathlessly. The fragile thread of common sense took a serious knocking at that remark.

'Really.' Another of those smiles did all sorts of things to her nervous system. 'I think it was what drew me to you in the first place. I saw you, Brianna, and I did a double take. It never occurred to me that I would find myself entering a situation over which I had no control. Yes, I lied about who I was, but there was no intention to hurt you. I would never have done that… *would* never do that.'

'You wouldn't?'

'Never,' he said with urgent sincerity. 'I was just passing through then we slept together and I ended up staying on.'

'To find out as much as you could about Bridget.'

'To be with you.'

Hope fluttered into life and Brianna found that she was holding her breath.

'I didn't even realise that I was sinking deeper and deeper. I was so accustomed to not committing when it came to relationships that I didn't recognise the signs. I told myself that I was just having time out, that you were a novelty I was temporarily enjoying but that, yes, I'd still be moving on.'

'And then you met her.'

'I met her and all my easy black-and-white notions flew through the window. This wasn't the lowlife who had jettisoned a baby without any conscience. This was a living, breathing human being with complexities I had never banked on, who overturned all the boxes I had been prepared to stick her in. I wanted to get to know her more. At the back of my mind—no, scratch that, at the forefront of my mind—I knew that I had dug a hole for myself with that innocuous lie I had told in the very beginning—and you know something? I couldn't have chosen a more inappropriate occupation for myself. Reading fiction is not my thing, never mind writing it. I didn't like myself for what I was doing, but I squashed that guilty, sickening feeling. It wasn't easy.'

'And then Bridget had that fall and...'

'And my cover was blown. It's strange, but most women would have been delighted to have discovered that the guy they thought was broke actually was a billionaire; they would happily have overlooked the "starving writer" facade and climbed aboard the "rich businessman" bandwagon. I'm sorry I lied to you, and I'm sorry I wasn't smart enough to come clean when I had the chance. I guess I knew that, if there was one woman on the planet who would rather the struggling writer than the rich businessman, it was you...'

Brianna shrugged.

'And, God, I'm sorry that I continued to stick to my facade long after it had become redundant... I seem to be apologising a heck of a lot.' His beautiful mouth curved into a rueful, self-deprecatory smile.

'And you don't do apologies.'

'Bingo.'

'What do you mean about sticking to your facade after it had become redundant?'

'I mean you laid into me like an avenging angel when you found out the truth about my identity and what did I do? I decided that nothing was going to change; that you might be upset, and we might have had a good thing going, but it didn't change the fact that I wasn't going to get wrapped up in justifying myself. Old habits die hard.'

He sighed and said, half to himself, 'When you walked out of my life, I let you go and it was the biggest mistake I ever made but pride wouldn't allow me to change my mind.'

'Biggest mistake?' Brianna said encouragingly.

'You're enjoying this, aren't you?' He slanted a glance at her that held lingering amusement.

'Err...'

'I can't say I blame you. We should go inside.'

'We can't sit on anything, Leo. We're both filthy. I don't think the owners would like it if we destroyed their lovely furniture with our muddy clothes.'

'My car, then. I assure you that that particular owner won't mind if the seats get dirty.' He stood up, flexed his muscles and then held out his hand for her to take.

She took it and felt that powerful current pass between them, fast, strong and invisible, uniting them. He pulled her up as though she weighed nothing and together they walked towards his car, making sure that the house was firmly locked before they left and the key returned to its original hiding place.

'No one living in London would ever dare to be so trusting,' he said, still holding her hand. She hadn't pulled away and he was weak enough to read that as a good sign.

'And no one where I live would ever be suspicious.'

He wanted to tell her that that was good, that if she chose to marry him, to share her life with him, she would be living somewhere safe, a place where neighbours trusted one another. If he could have disassociated himself from his extravagantly expensive penthouse apartment, he would have.

She insisted that they put something on the seats and he obliged by fetching a rug from the trunk, one of the many things which Harry had insisted would come in handy some day but for which he had never before had any use. Then he opened the back door of the car so that he wasn't annoyed by a gear box separating them.

Brianna stepped in and said something frivolous about back seats of cars, which she instantly regretted, because didn't everyone know what the back seats of cars were used for?

'But you liked the house; you said so.' Had he mentioned that before? Was he dredging up an old, tired argument which she had already rejected? 'It's more than just the house, Brianna, and it's more than just marriage because it makes sense. It's even bigger than my past, bigger than me wanting to do right by this child because of what happened to me when I was a baby.' He rested back and sought out her hand without looking at her.

Brianna squeezed his fingers tentatively and was reassured when he returned the gesture.

'If you hadn't shown up, if you hadn't sought me out to tell me about the pregnancy, I would have eventually come for you because you were more than just a passing relationship. I may have wanted to keep you in that box, but you climbed out of it and I couldn't stuff you back in and, hell, I tried.' He laughed ruefully. 'Like I said, old habits die hard.'

'It means a lot for you to say that you would have come for me,' Brianna said huskily. They weren't looking at one another but the connection was still thrumming between their clasped fingers.

'I wouldn't have had a choice, Brianna. Because I need you, and I love you, and I can't imagine any kind of life without you in it. I think I've known that for a long time, but I just didn't admit it to myself. I've never been in love with any one before, so what were my points of comparison? Without a shred of vanity, I will admit that life's been good to me. Everything I touched turned to gold, but I finally realised that none of the gold was worth a damn when the only woman I've ever loved turned her back on me.'

Brianna had soared from ground level to cloud nine in the space of a heartbeat.

'You *love* me?'

'Which is why marriage may not make sense to you, but it makes sense to me. Which is why all the ingredients are there…for me.'

'Why didn't you say?' She twisted to face him and flung her arms around his neck, which was an awkward position, because they were sitting alongside one another. But as she adjusted her body, so did he, until they were face to face, chest to chest, body pressed tightly against body. Now she was sure that she could feel his heart beating, matching hers.

'I love you so much,' she whispered shakily. 'When you proposed, all I could think was that you were doing it because it was the sensible option, and I didn't want us to be married because it was a sensible option. If I hadn't loved you so much, Leo, maybe I would have jumped at the chance—but I knew that if you didn't love me back that road would only end up leading to heartbreak.'

His mouth found hers and they kissed urgently and passionately, holding on to one another as if their lives depended on it.

'I've never felt anything like this before…' The feel of her against him was like a minor miracle. He wanted just to keep holding her for ever. 'And I didn't have the vocabulary to tell you how I felt. The only thing I could do was hope that my actions spoke on my behalf and, when they didn't, when I thought that I was going to lose everything...'

'You came out there...' She reached up and sighed with pleasure as their mouths met yet again, this time with lingering tenderness. She smoothed her fingers over his face and then through his hair, enjoying the familiarity of the sensation.

'So...' he said gravely. Even though he was ninety-nine per cent certain of the answer she would give him, he still feared that one per cent response he might hear. This, he thought, was what love felt like. It made you open and vulnerable to another person. It turned wanting into needing and self-control into a roller-coaster ride. He could think of nowhere he would rather have been.

'Yes. Yes, yes, yes! I'll marry you.'

'When?' Leo demanded and Brianna laughed with pleasure.

'When do you think? A girl needs time to plan these things, you know...'

'Would two weeks be time enough?'

She laughed again and looked at him tenderly. 'More than enough time!'

But in the end, it was six long weeks before they tied the knot in the little local church not a million miles away from her pub. The entire community turned out for the bash and, with typical Irish exuberance, the extremely happily wedded couple were not allowed to leave until for their honeymoon until the following morning.

They left a very proud Bridget behind to oversee the running of the pub because Ireland was her home in the end and she had been reluctant to leave it behind for good.

'But expect a very frequent visitor,' she had said to Brianna.

Brianna didn't doubt it. The older woman had rediscovered a joy for living ever since Leo had appeared on the scene, ever since she had rediscovered the baby, now a man, whom she had been compelled to give away at such a young age. She had spent her life existing under a dark cloud from which there had been no escape, she had confided to Brianna,. The cloud had now gone. Being asked to do the job of overseeing the pub, which had been signed over to her, was the icing on the cake.

Now, nearly two days after their wedding, Brianna sat on the veranda of their exquisite beach villa, a glass of orange juice in her hand and her baby bump a little bigger than when she had first headed down to London with a madly beating heart to break the news of her pregnancy to the man who she could hear padding out to join her.

The past few weeks had been the happiest of

her life. By the time they returned to England, the house which she had loved on sight would be theirs and what lay ahead glittered like a pathway paved in precious jewels: a life with the man she adored; a man who never tired of telling her how much he loved her; a baby which would be the perfect celebration of their love. And not forgetting Bridget, a true member of their family.

'What are you thinking?'

Brianna smiled and looked up at him. The sun had already set and the sea was a dark, still mass lapping against the sand. It was warm and the sound of myriad insects was harmonious background music: the Caribbean at its most perfect.

'I'm thinking that this must be what paradise is like.'

'Sun, sand and sea but without the alcoholic cocktails?' Leo teased, swinging round so that he could sit next to her and place his hand on her swollen stomach. He marvelled that he never seemed to tire of feeling the baby move. He was awestruck that he was so besotted with her, that he hated her being out of sight, that work, which had hitherto been his driving force, had taken a back seat.

'That's exactly right.' Brianna laughed and then her eyes flared as he slipped his hand under the loose cotton dress so that now it rested directly on her stomach, dipping below the swell to cup her between her legs.

'Have I told you how sexy I find your pregnant body?' he murmured into her ear.

'You may have once or twice, or more!' She lay back, as languorous as a cat, and smiled when he gave a low grunt of pleasure.

'And now...' he kissed the lobe of her ear and felt her smile broaden '...I think there are more pressing things for us to do than watch the sea, don't you?'

He could have added that he too now knew what paradise felt like.

* * * * *